The Loner

Stu Campbell

This is a work of fiction.

ISBN: 978-0-9988499-0-4

6   5   4   3   2   1

Edited by Mira Perrizo
Cover and text design by D.K. Luraas
Cover illustration by R. Loren Schmidt

Printed in the United States of America

Contents

Getting Hired

"Can you buckaroo?"

The question caught me by surprise. I wasn't sure what a buckaroo was. I knew what a cowboy was, I figured myself to be a pretty good hand around the ranch. I'd done everything I'd been asked, from the horseback jobs to the irrigating to the hay cutting and baling to fixing fence. But I didn't know what a buckaroo was.

Not sure what I was getting myself into, I answered, "I guess so."

The man who asked the question eyed me suspiciously. "We're short of help, we can use you for a few days, if you can ride."

I didn't have a problem riding and figured myself a pretty good rider. "I'm short of money, so I can help you out for a few days."

"We have to gather about seven hundred head of cows along with their calves and move them to the winter range. We'll be a day gathering cattle and two days trailing them. We can use you for the three days. After that, we're essentially done 'til spring. We have enough help to sort off the calves later."

"I can help you for the three days. It'll help me out some," I said.

"We're a little short of horses, but we can get you two horses. That will be all you need for three days. One of 'em is kinda green, can you handle him?"

"I guess so. We'll find out."

"The green horse is started and started in a hackamore. You got one?"

"Yep," I answered.

I liked using a hackamore. We started all our colts at home

1

in a hackamore, and the stud we had never had a bit in his mouth. All he'd been ridden in was a hackamore. I thought I was pretty well educated in their use.

The next question surprised me. "You got your own saddle and equipment?"

"Yep," I said, trying to conceal my surprise. "An' I got my own hackamore too." I was kinda excited about getting a job and repeated myself.

I'd bought a saddle a few years previously. It was a George W. Lawrence saddle, out of Oregon. It had what they call an "improved association" tree. I liked it and it was the only saddle I rode. I'd only paid fifty bucks for it and figured it to be a good investment.

I had a few city friends, going to school in town, but not many. A few of them would ask, "Do you have a horse?"

"Nope," I would answer.

"If you don't have a horse, how come you have a saddle?" they would reply.

My answer was standard. "With my own saddle, I can always get a job. I can't necessarily get a job with a horse."

Often, I was tempted to answer, "I use the saddle to sit in when I'm watching western movies on television. Then I can become part of the action," but never said that. It might have been interesting to watch their reaction to that answer.

I was told to put my bedroll in the bunkhouse and just hang out until supper, so I did.

At supper, I ate with the other buckaroos. We ate separately from the other ranch hands and I wondered if buckaroos were a separate class of people, perhaps above or below the others. I came to find out that buckaroos were a separate class of people and they figured themselves to be above everyone else. Most everybody else figured them the same way.

I was curious to find out about the horses I'd be riding during my brief stay at this outfit. But I didn't ask any questions.

The next morning, the cow boss came through the bunk-house waking everyone up. I was surprised he'd do that; on most cow outfits, the hands were used to getting up early and didn't need to be rousted out. But I'd noticed at supper the night before that the buckaroos were all older men. I wondered if the word buckaroo meant too old to do anything else.

The cow boss roped out everyone's horse from the cavy. When he gave me the horse he'd picked for me to ride, he said as I haltered him, "You might want to hobble him before you saddle him. I'll give you a hand after I get my horse saddled."

I did have a set of hobbles, although I hadn't used them much. At home we spent a lot of time working the colts we were breaking on the ground, getting them used to being handled by humans.

I took the horse, hobbled him and saddled him. He was a little skittish when I saddled him, but I got the job done. The cow boss looked a little surprised when he came over to help me and found out I didn't need any help.

Satisfied that I was managing well, he said, "Make sure you untrack him before you get on!"

I had the feeling that I was being treated like a "green" hand but didn't say anything. I had a job for a few days and it meant I could eat for a few days and would have enough money to travel on and find a winter job.

I untracked the horse, cheeked him and got on. I always cheeked a strange horse when I got on him the first time. "Cheeking" a horse means taking a hold of the headstall and pulling the horse's head toward you when you get on. By pull-ing his head when you're getting on, the horse can only turn toward you, making it easier to get on. A feller can also keep the horse's head up, preventing him from bucking while he's getting on.

I was busy getting on and didn't notice if the other bucka-roos approved or not. But I did notice them all watching me after I mounted. I let the horse stand for a moment and gently slid back and forth in the saddle, shifting the saddle a little. The horse took a step or two to the side, but didn't offer to buck or do anything else.

The cow boss was watching and when everyone was mounted, said, "Let's go, boys!" There were only four of us, five counting the cow boss. I fell in behind the cow boss and the other four followed us. I wondered if they were following me just to watch what would happen if something happened.

My horse started out a little unsteady, like he wasn't sure what he was supposed to do. The cow boss started out at a walk and when we got outside the yard of the ranch, he increased his gait to a trot. My horse humped up a little at being asked to trot, but a sharp tug on the hackamore made him pay attention. After we'd trotted a mile or so, my horse settled down and I could feel him relax a little under the saddle.

One of the older buckaroos rode up alongside me and said, "You seem to be gettin' along pretty good with that horse."

"Yep," I said. "I think he wants to be a good horse. What do you call him?"

"They've been calling him Rowdy, along with a few other choice names. He's bucked a few of the other boys off. I don't think he's very trustworthy. Just watch him."

"I will," I said.

After about two more miles, we got to a big grass pasture. The cow boss opened the wire gate, let everyone through, closed the gate, got back on his horse and gave everyone instructions.

"Be sure you ride the willows along the creek good. We don't want to leave anything. Take everything to the east. I'll count 'em through the gate. Then all we have to do is follow them along the road."

We went to the west with the cow boss, dropping off a buckaroo when there were some cows to gather. He told the other

4

hands, "Be sure and wait until we have a chance to push the cows out of the creek bottom." Finally, it was just the cow boss and me.

"You ride this side of the creek, I'll take the other. I gave the other hands the easier parts to gather. They're a little older, and you've got plenty of horse. What cows you find along the creek, push them out to the other guys up on the flat. They'll pick 'em up. I'll push what cows I find over to you and you can move 'em with the others. They can pick 'em up. This should be a pretty easy gather."

We separated and started our gather. I could hear the cow boss hollering at a few cows, his language sprinkled with some colorful adjectives and saw a few cows crossing the creek. Soon, I had about fifty cows and looked for a convenient place to move them out of the creek bottom. Some of the cows had found an appropriate place and had already started out of the creek bottom and I decided to move everything I had up on top.

I followed the cows out of the creek bottom and was surprised to see the other hands about a quarter mile ahead of me, pushing a small bunch of cows east. They hadn't waited as they were told to. I hollered real loud and saw one of the hands turn around. He started back toward me and I waited until he showed up to take charge of the cattle I had.

When he arrived, at a trot, he said, "You've got more cattle than we do."

"Yep," I said. "You guys might want to slow down some. There's a lot of cattle in the bottom and it ain't easy. It's a little tough gettin' 'em out of the willows."

"Yeah," said the old timer.

I thought I detected a note of animosity in his voice. Perhaps he didn't like being told what to do by someone considerably younger than himself.

Oh well, I thought. *We have a job to do and I won't let his thoughts about me personally interfere with me doing my job.*

Without another word, he started moving the cows I'd brought out of the bottom toward the cattle they'd already gathered. I returned to the creek bottom and was surprised to see the cow boss waiting on my side of the creek.

"Where you been?" he asked.

"I moved the cows we found out on top only to find the other boys hadn't waited. They were about a quarter mile ahead of me. I had to get their attention before I could come back. But they've got the cows now."

Disgustedly, the cow boss spat out some tobacco juice and said, "That Jess! Never had much patience. Always wanting to rush things! We'll continue and if we have to, we'll wait for them to come back for the cattle we find."

He left without another word and I waited until I could hear him yelling at some cows. Then I started and gathered the cattle the cow boss had pushed toward me and the cows on my side of the creek. We continued along the creek for about another half a mile and I found a place where I could move the cattle out on top. I was surprised to see the other hands waiting for me. They took the cows I found, mixed them with what they already had and I returned to the creek bottom.

At one point, something set off my horse and he started to buck. I couldn't pull his head up to get him to stop bucking. For all practical purposes he had me bucked off and I was pulling leather for all I was worth. Then, all of the sudden, he stopped. One more jump and I was sure I was going to hit the ground. But I lucked out and was still in the saddle!

We continued that way until the creek bottom opened up into the grass pasture. I could see the other hands and cattle ahead of me, and the cow boss was pushing a bunch of cattle off to my right. There was no need to move the cattle off the creek bottom, as it opened onto the pasture.

Before we got to the gate, the cow boss rode up to me and said, "What set off Rowdy?"

"I don't know," I said. "Maybe a willow branch tickled him or something, I don't know."

"He had you all but bucked off. I saw it all and actually enjoyed it," the cow boss said.

"I was too busy to enjoy it," I said. "I all but pulled my saddle horn off!"

The cow boss laughed. "Those George W. Lawrence saddles are made good! You watch that horse, there's no telling what he'll do or when. I won't say anything to the other boys. I haven't been able to get any of them to ride him. If they think you got along okay with him, maybe I can get someone else to ride him. He's too good a horse to get rid of. He just needs a lot of riding. Don't you say anything!"

"Wet saddle blankets makes a lot of good horses," I said. "But I'll keep my mouth shut."

He didn't say anything else and rode off.

At the gate, the cow boss opened it and started counting the cattle through it. He motioned for one of the other hands to move up closer to him to regulate how many cows were moving through the gate at one time. The rest of us just held the main herd.

When the last cow had passed through the gate, the cow boss wrote his numbers down then moved to the head of the herd. He had Jess accompany him. "We need to slow down the leaders!" he said. "They know where they're going!"

Along the way, Jess told the cow boss, "We left a lame cow back there. She'll never make it to the winter pasture."

"We'll come back with the truck and trailer and get her later," said the cow boss.

One hand took the right side of the herd and another one took the left side. I was left with the other hand to bring up the rear, riding drag. There was a lot of dust and in the old days, the drag was generally left to the more inexperienced hands. But I didn't mind. I was getting a wage and riding the drag would give Rowdy more work. For every mile we moved east, Rowdy probably had to travel a mile north and south keeping up the stragglers. He had more work to do.

I found out the name of the other hand that was riding the drag with me. It was Lester. He didn't have much to say. I didn't know if I had been accepted by the other buckaroos or not, but it didn't make much difference.

We reached a holding pasture and the cattle were turned into it for the night. There was a truck and trailer waiting to take us back to the ranch.

At supper, the cow boss said, "Tomorrow we'll take the cattle and move them closer to the winter range. We'll be on the road most of the way. We'll just have to make sure the gates along the road are closed and we keep the cows from going into someone's driveway. Jess and I will ride up front. Stan, you and Terry, you both know the road, you block off the driveways on either side and you and Lester bring up the rear."

It occurred to me that no one had referred to me by my name. I'd introduced myself to the cow boss when I applied for the job. *That's fine,* I thought. *I won't be here that long anyway!*

The next day the cow boss gave me a different horse. I was a little disappointed, Rowdy was becoming a good horse and I thought he'd become better with more riding. But it was the custom to use a horse only once in his turn in the string.

"We call this guy Diamond," said the cow boss as I haltered the horse. "You can ride him with a curb bit or a hackamore. He's a little more dependable than Rowdy."

"I'll use a hackamore on him. I won't have to dig out a bridle."

I hobbled the horse and noticed the way he was standing. I thought he'd been foundered. Before I saddled him, I asked the cow boss, "Has this horse been foundered? Look at the way he's standing."

The cow boss looked at the horse. "There's a lot of conditions that can make a horse stand that way, looking like he's been foundered. I figure he's got bowed tendons. He'll act like he's lame for a little bit, but when he warms up, he'll be all right."

"Shouldn't his legs be wrapped or something?" I asked.

"Probably, but he'll be all right."

Apprehensively, I saddled the horse.

I cheeked the horse as I got on and Lester said, "You don't have to cheek that horse."

But I was already on, having cheeked the horse and swung into the saddle. I rode him around a little and felt a little disgusted that I'd been given a lame horse to ride. I got off and we loaded the horses into the trailer to ride to the holding pasture.

We gathered the holding pasture and although Diamond acted like he was lame for the first few minutes, he gradually worked out of it.

I saw that Jess was riding a flashy paint horse and thought he'd picked that horse to ride so as he'd be noticed by anyone driving along the highway. That was the case. He willingly posed for any of the late season tourists that asked for his picture.

The day was pretty easy. With fences on both sides of the highway most of the way, there wasn't much to do other than keep the cattle moving. It actually turned out to be a pretty boring day.

We got the herd to another holding pasture and turned them loose. The cow boss left us and went back for the truck. The rest of us got off our horses, hobbled them and sat down. Two of the boys stretched out like they were going to take a nap. There wasn't much conversation while we waited for the truck and trailer.

Someone asked me, "You don't say much, do you?"

"Nope," I answered. "I don't want to wake them other fellers up!"

There was a loud "Ha!" from one of the guys stretched out with his hat over his eyes.

The cow boss returned, we loaded the horses and returned

to the ranch. At supper, the cow boss said, "We should have the cattle where they belong by mid-afternoon tomorrow. Then we'll be done."

The following day I was given Rowdy to ride again. Knowing what I had, I hobbled him, saddled him, took off the hobbles, untracked him and got on, cheeking him as I did. He was a little nervous and I rode him around just to take off the edge. He'd had a day to think about being ridden.

Although I didn't say anything, I thought if he bucked me off, he'd be easier to catch around the home ranch. But he didn't offer to buck and we loaded him and the other horses in the truck and drove to where we'd left the cattle yesterday.

We gathered the cattle and put them on the road with everyone taking the same positions they'd had yesterday. The day was again boring and we turned the cattle loose on water on their winter range. The cow boss left early to get the truck and trailer and Jess turned the cattle onto the winter range.

Rowdy hadn't offered to misbehave at all during the day. He was becoming a good horse.

We returned to the ranch. The cow boss told me, "We're done. After you get your stuff loaded, come to the office and I'll pay you off."

I put my saddle, blankets, and hackamore in the car. I noticed that the other hands gathered around as I loaded my equipment. I thought they were going to say goodbye, but they never said a word. It occurred to me later that they had gathered around just to make sure I wasn't going to steal any of their equipment.

I put my bedroll in the car and went to the office to get my wages. I found the cow boss waiting for me.

"I appreciate your help," he said, as he handed me my pay envelope. "There's an extra twenty in there, for the good job you did of riding Rowdy. I wish we could keep you on, but right now we've hardly got enough work for the old pensioners we have."

I took the check and said, "Thanks! I appreciate the extra. That Rowdy horse will make a good horse with more riding. I think I'd ride him two days in a row, give him a day off, then two more days of riding. If he was rotated like that for a spell he'd be okay."

The cow boss gave me a funny look as if to say, "Who are you telling me how to run my outfit?"

But he just uttered a "Yeah." Then he added, "If you're around in the spring, about calving time, check back with me. We might could use some more help then."

Without committing, I said, "Yeah."

We shook hands and I left. I didn't know where I was going, but I did have a little money. I thought, with winter coming, I might want to head farther south, where it might be warmer. But I did stop at the first town that had an employment office to see if anyone needed some help for a few days.

There were a few ranchers looking for help to put the rest of their hay up, but I wasn't much interested in that.

I asked the employment counselor, "Is anyone looking for a buckaroo for a few days or weeks?"

"There's one outfit. They've been short of help all fall. They have a hard time keeping help."

The counselor's last comment should have warned me, but I wasn't paying attention. "Who's the cow boss?" I asked.

"There's not a cow boss. The owner runs things," was the reply.

Again, I should have listened, but didn't.

"Where is it and how do you get there?" I asked.

The counselor wrote down instructions and handed them to me. Then he wrote out what he called a recommendation and said, "This will introduce you to the owner. He'll probably hire you, although the last few people we've sent out only stayed a few days."

I said, "Thank you," took the papers and left for the ranch. I thought, *If I hurry, I can probably get there in time for supper.* I got to the turnoff to the ranch and noticed that there was about three or four inches of dust on the road.

I should have gotten something to eat while I was in town. When I got to the ranch, I met the owner and got hired. The owner was a short, fat man with a gruff manner. To me, he looked too fat to ride.

The owner said, "If you go to the cook shack, you might get something to eat, although I think they've finished. The cook's name is Cecil. Tell him I hired you. Put your bedroll in the bunkhouse. We'll start at five in the morning with breakfast."

I went to the cook shack. The cook was the only one there and he was doing dishes. I noticed a bottle of cheap wine, about half gone, on the windowsill above the sink. I thought that was strange. Cow outfits didn't generally allow liquor on the ranch.

"You Cecil?" I asked.

"Yep," replied the cook, half way turning to see who it was.

"The boss just hired me and sent me over," I said. "He said maybe I could get a little supper.

"Supper's over. There's some coffee left if you want it."

I thought it strange the cook didn't even offer me some leftovers. I got what looked to be the cleanest cup and poured some coffee, sat down at the table and looked the kitchen over.

In one corner I saw what appeared to be a brown saddle blanket. *That's an interesting decoration for the kitchen,* I thought.

Upon closer inspection, I decided it wasn't a saddle blanket. It was a spider web, the biggest one I'd ever seen! The brown color came from all the dust that had collected on it during the years.

"What can you tell me about this outfit?" I asked.

"Not much," said Cecil as he continued to do the dishes. "Just another small cow outfit."

Cecil didn't seem too talkative and I didn't ask any more questions. When he finished the dishes he went to his bedroom, which was off of the kitchen. He took the half bottle of wine with him.

"Make sure you clean your cup when you're done," he said as he entered the bedroom and closed the door.

I began to wonder what I'd gotten myself into. When I finished my coffee, I cleaned the cup. I thought it was cleaner than it was when I first poured coffee in it when I got done. I went to my car, got my bedroll and went to the bunkhouse. There were only two hands in there, both of them stretched out on their bunks.

"New hand, huh?" stated one of the hands. "Put your bedroll over there on one of the empty bunks."

I did as I was told and after I unrolled it, I turned to get acquainted with the other buckaroos. They were both asleep on their bunks, in their working clothes. They both appeared to be older.

I looked them over and thought they were both old enough that they needed their sleep, so I didn't wake them to make conversation.

I went to bed hungry and wondering just what I'd gotten myself into. I actually wondered if I ought to take my saddle, bridles and chaps out of the car.

The next morning, I was up and dressed earlier than the other two hands. I was hungry and went to the cook shack early.

"Breakfast ain't until five," said the cook.

I looked at my watch. It was ten till.

"Coffee ready?" I asked.

"Five," was the short reply from the cook.

I went to my car, got my saddle, blankets, a halter, a snaffle bit, and my chaps. I didn't need my spurs, they were already on my boots. I kept them on all the time when I was riding. I took my equipment to the corral where the horses were and looked over the small bunch of horses in it. I wondered what I'd be riding.

Looking over the horses, I decided there wasn't anything there that particularly stood out.

I kept an eye on the bunkhouse and when I saw the other hands leave for the cook shack, I followed them.

"How do you want your eggs?" asked one the hands as I entered the cook shack.

"Any way," I answered. "I'm not particular."

"Scrambled is how you'll get 'em," said the cook.

I got my scrambled eggs, some bacon and sat down to eat. Breakfast was eaten in silence. Nobody introduced themself to me and I remained silent. I noticed a new bottle of wine on the windowsill.

I didn't think much of the breakfast, but was too hungry to complain.

After breakfast, we went to the corral. The owner was there, looking over my saddle that I'd put on the top rail of the corral.

"Pretty old saddle," said the owner.

"Yep," I said, "but it's in good condition. Serviceable."

"You ride that little sorrel over there," he said.

I started to get my rope from the saddle, but the owner stopped me. "You don't need to rope him, you can catch him on foot." he said.

I took the halter, caught the horse, hobbled and saddled him. He seemed gentle enough as I did this. Then I swung into the saddle, cheeking the horse. He didn't do anything.

The owner, watching this, said, "He's gentle enough. My fourteen-year-old daughter rides him."

The other two hands were mounted. The owner told us where he wanted us to go. "I'll meet you on top of the ridge," he said.

"How's he goin' to get up there if he don't have a horse?" I asked.

"He'll meet us up there in the truck," answered one of the hands. "By the way, what's your name? I'm Chet."

I told him my name and he said, "That other guy is Tony. We went to sleep last night before we could get acquainted."

"How come the owner is goin' in the truck?" I asked.

"He don't ride," said Chet. "Says he used to, but I don't believe it. I think he's been too fat all his life to ride."

"Probably," I said. "How's he able to tell what's happenin'?"

"He sits up on top of the ridges with a pair of binoculars so he can see what's happening," replied Chet.

We started out and met the owner on top of the ridge where we were supposed to. He told each rider where he wanted us to go and where he'd seen cattle. And he told us where we'd meet him.

We started out following the instructions we'd been given. We gathered cattle along the way and met where we were supposed to. The owner was there, waiting for us, sipping on a bottle of whisky. To me, he looked about half drunk, but he managed to give further instructions to us fairly coherently. When he was done, he said, "See you back at the ranch, fellers."

We did as we were told and when done, rode back to the ranch.

On the way back, Tony said, "I hope Cecil has supper ready when we get there. It's been a long time since breakfast."

I checked my watch. It was only two o'clock

"We'll probably have to wait again," said Chet. "I imagine he's probably workin' on that other bottle of wine by now."

We got back to the ranch about three o'clock, grained and turned our horses loose and went to the bunkhouse. Chet went to the cook shack to see when supper would be ready.

When he returned to the bunkhouse, he said, "Supper will be ready in about fifteen minutes."

"What is it tonight?" asked Tony. "Same as last night?"

"Yep. Stew again."

"I'm sure gettin' tired of stew," said Tony. "Don't he know how to cook anythin' else?"

"I don't think so," replied Chet.

We ate an early supper and went to the bunkhouse.

Later, the owner came to the bunkhouse and said, "Tomorrow we'll gather the other side of the mountain. I won't be along to help, I've got too much work to do in the office. But you boys know the country, you shouldn't have any trouble without me."

His words were slurred and to me he was obviously inebriated, probably hung over from the day before.

"Chet, have this new guy ride Sleepy. You can point him out to him tomorrow." He left.

The boss had forgotten my name. I wasn't surprised.

"Well," said Tony, "we won't have him along tomorrow. That'll be kind of a relief. He hasn't done anything but sit in the truck an' holler at us since I been here!"

"We'll get along okay," said Chet. "I'll tell Cecil that we expect to be done a little early tomorrow. We might get supper on time for a change."

"Not if Cecil an' the owner sit around drinkin' all day," said Tony. "It'll just be stew again anyways."

I didn't say anything during the conversation between Chet and Tony. I just listened and had more misgivings about what I'd gotten myself into.

Breakfast was at five the next morning. I made sure I was there on time—not early or late. The eggs were scrambled again and I thought the bacon was warmed over from the day before.

That morning, Chet pointed out Sleepy to me and I caught him. "Don't let the name fool you," he said as I saddled the horse.

I was familiar with how horses were named out on Nevada cow outfits. Often, plumb gentle horses were given notorious sounding names and real rank horses were named after fairy tale characters out of children's books.

"He's really a good gentle horse," Chet added as he noticed my look of apprehension.

I untracked the horse, cheeked him and got on. The horse didn't offer to do anything and all day he did just what I asked him. I didn't have any trouble with him at all.

We gathered cattle all day and left them close to where we'd left the cattle we'd gathered the day before. When we got back to the ranch, the owner and Cecil were sitting on the front porch of the house, drinking.

When Cecil saw us approaching, he got up and staggered to the cook shack. "Supper's ready," he said. "All I have to do is warm it up!"

"Stew again!" muttered Tony.

We ate supper. When we were done, Cecil said to me, "The owner wants to talk to you over at the big house."

I went to the house, wondering what the owner wanted. I didn't think I'd done anything worthy of being fired for. *Oh, well,* I thought, *if he fires me, that's fine. I'm ready to leave anyway!*

"I have a favor to ask of you," said the owner.

"Shoot," I said.

"My daughter has to go back to school. Can you take her to town so she can catch a bus? I still have a lot of paperwork to do."

"I suppose so. When does she have to be there?" I thought to myself, *He probably realizes he's too drunk to drive.*

"Tonight, by nine," replied the owner.

"Have her ready in an hour an' we'll go to town," I said.

Taking the owner's daughter to town wasn't really part of the buckaroo job description, but I did it anyway. The ride to the bus station was quiet. The girl didn't say anything and I was content to remain silent.

We got to the bus station and I waited while she bought her ticket and waited until she got on the bus and left. I didn't think it was right to leave her alone at the bus station.

Driving back to the ranch, I decided to leave the place the

next day. I'd help out during the day, draw my pay after the work was done and leave. I wasn't too impressed with the outfit.

I always kinda dreaded leaving a job. I didn't know what to say and really didn't want to give out the real reasons for my leaving. But I didn't think there was any kind of a future on that outfit.

Driving down the dusty road to the ranch, I had the thought that all the dust was caused by all the other help leaving the ranch. The employment counselor had told me that this outfit had a hard time keeping help. I could see why, with the dirty kitchen, the same old stew every day, a drunken, surly cook and an owner that didn't do anything except from his truck.

Having made up my mind what I was going to do, I slept soundly that night. The next morning, I told the owner, "I've decided I'm goin' to roll up an' move on when we get done this afternoon."

The owner paused. Finally, he said, "Okay. I'll have your check ready when you get back to the ranch." Apparently he was used to having his hired help leave on a moment's notice.

I was given the little sorrel horse to ride that I'd rode the first day I was on the job. We gathered the cattle that we'd rounded up the two days before and moved them onto the winter range. The owner was at the gate and counted the cattle through it.

"Come to the house when you're done. Your check will be ready when you get back to the ranch," he said before he drove off in the truck.

As we rode back to the ranch, Chet asked me, "You leavin'?"

I hadn't said anything about my plans to anyone during the day. "Yep," I said.

"How come?" asked Tony.

Rather than telling the whole truth about why I was leaving, I just said, "I don't think there's much of a future for me here." That was true enough. The other guys already knew how bad the food was.

We got to the ranch and I unsaddled my horse by the car and put my saddle, blankets, and other equipment in the trunk. I went to the ranch and got my paycheck. I checked it when I got in the car to leave. It was all there, but he hadn't reimbursed me for the gas I'd used to take his daughter to town. I thought I ought to go say something, but then thought better of it. I was glad to be leaving.

I drove to the bunkhouse to get my bedroll and Chet asked me, "Ain't you goin' to stay for supper?"

"Nope," I said. "I'll get something good to eat in town."

Tony came up and said, "Where you goin? I wish I was goin' with you."

"I don't know where I'm headed. Someplace where it will be warmer during the winter."

I shook hands with Chet and Tony. "Good luck," I said.

"Yeah, same to you," was their reply.

Drifting

I drove off the ranch, thinking I would be adding more dust to that left by the other hands. I thought that would be the last time I would go either direction on that road.

I got into town and had a big T-bone steak at the first steakhouse I came to. It was sure a lot better than the stew I'd been fed. I was sure some of the ingredients in that stew had been in there for a couple of weeks.

I got a motel room and got a good long, hot shower and some clean clothes. I hadn't realized how much dust I'd accumulated. The next morning, I went to the employment office to look for work.

There was a position available on the ranch I'd just left. I didn't tell them I'd just left that ranch. "I'm goin' the other direction," I said.

"There are some sheep herding positions available farther south," said the lady at the employment office.

"I'm not interested in herding sheep all winter," I replied. "I'd like a little more action than that."

"All we have available is some hay hauling jobs in the agricultural field. Maybe you'd like something in town for the winter? There are a lot of jobs available, bartending and the like."

"I'm not interested in spending the winter in town," I said. "I'll just go farther south until I find something."

I drove farther south for the next couple of days. The country was desolate and to save money, I camped out. The first night I camped, I went without supper. I'd forgot to get some groceries when I went through the last town.

The following day, I got some canned beans at the grocery store. I passed on the canned stew. I also bought some soda pop and some plastic knives, forks, and spoons. Now I was better prepared to camp alongside the road.

I noticed the country changing the farther south I went. It was becoming drier and the grass was becoming scarcer. I wondered how many acres it took to feed a cow for a month in this country. *Plenty*, I thought.

I came to a town and checked at the employment agency. I was told there was a position available on a dude ranch.

"I've never done any of that kind of work," I said.

"It's pretty easy," said the counselor. "Just saddle horses and take the dudes out on rides through the desert. Of course, they don't call them dudes, they call them guests. The wages are low, but you can make more money in tips. If I were you, I'd give it a try."

"Tell me how to get there, I'll go talk to them."

I was given instructions on how to get to the dude ranch and told who to ask for. "Steve, he's the manager. The place is owned by a movie star and he's rarely there."

I went to the ranch. The road into the headquarters was dirt, but well maintained. There wasn't as much dust on the road as there had been on the other place. I was surprised when I got to the main ranch. The buildings were well maintained, there were pathways between the buildings and the grass was kept short. The barn was neat and orderly. The horses were all in good shape from what I could tell.

I found Steve and got acquainted. He was a pleasant fellow, not surly or gruff like the hands on the last place I'd worked.

"What's your experience?" he asked.

"I've been cowboyin' an' buckarooin' up north," I said.

"Who for?"

I named off the outfits I'd worked for in Utah, Montana, and Nevada. I was careful not to mention the last place I'd worked for.

"We could probably use you, but not for another month,"

said Steve. "The guests don't start showing up until then, when it starts getting cold up north. Come back around the middle of November and you'll have a job. Taking care of the dudes might be a little tame for you after buckarooing, but we'll see how it goes."

I left feeling confident I had a job for the winter where it would be a little warmer, but didn't know what I'd do for the next three weeks or so. If I had to, I could go to the employment office and hire myself out as a day laborer. I could sleep in the back of my car and eat in restaurants. That was my only option.

I didn't have any luck the next day at the employment agency. There wasn't much of a demand for day laborers in that town. I thought I'd better try another town close by.

At the next town, I heard of a position helping out with tree trimming and yard maintenance. I got the address of the business and went to their office. Not having anything at all to do, and thinking more money might be a good thing, I applied, not knowing what I was getting myself into.

I was interviewed by the owner of the business, whose name was Seth. He was a nice fellow, dressed in casual work clothes.

"Can you operate a chainsaw?" he asked.

"Yep," I said, "although I haven't got much experience with one."

"Can you operate a lawn mower?"

"Ridin' or pushing?" I answered.

The owner laughed. "Mostly riding," he said. "What other kind of equipment can you operate?"

"I've run most farm equipment," I replied, "although it's been a while. I've been makin' a living from the back of a horse for the past few years. Ridin' jobs."

"A real cowboy," he said. "My wife's got horses. Really loves them. I get to pay the feed bill! They're really expensive! You got any horses?"

"Nope," I answered. "I find it's easier to get a job without one. And I won't own one unless I've got a job for him. I do have a job coming up in the middle of November, ridin' on a dude ranch. That's why I'm only lookin' for work for a few weeks."

"Well," said Seth, "we'll use you for a few days, just to see how it works out. You got a place to stay?"

"I'll stay in my car," I replied.

"You can park it here in the yard. Don't be going out and partying at night. I don't need any drunks working for me."

"Yes sir," I answered.

"There's a café down the road apiece where you can eat. They're open at six, although we don't get started here until eight. Be ready. I'll line you out in the morning.

The next day I was at the café early, got breakfast and went back to the yard to wait. Seth showed up about seven-thirty.

"Mornin'," I said.

"Good morning!" came Seth's reply. "It's going to be a great day!

His attitude was positive and he actually acted like he looked forward to going to work. Quite a change from the attitude that was on the last outfit I'd worked for.

Seth showed me how to operate the riding lawn mower. Then he showed me how to operate the edger.

"We use this to trim up the lawn next to sidewalks and driveways," he said. "Then we use this to trim around the trees, fence posts, and the like. We call it a weed eater. I got it so my wife could use it to shave her legs, but she didn't like the idea. That's how we got it," he said, laughing at his own humor.

I laughed at the joke also.

The other help started showing up.

"I'll take you out to our first job. They'll be two of you mowing the lawn. It'll take you both most of the morning to mow the lawn and do all the trimming. Dave will be with you, he knows the place. You'll follow me in his truck. When you get done, he knows where to go next."

We followed Seth to a gated property. He entered the code and the gate opened and we entered. The place looked more like a golf course than a residence. It was a mansion and I wondered if it belonged to the movie star I was supposed to work for later.

Seth gave me a quick walk through on the operation of a riding mower and left. Dave had already started his mower and I followed his lead. We were a couple of hours mowing the yard. When we were done, Dave gave me the weed eater and said, "You take this and trim around the trees, fence posts, and statues. I'll use the edger on the driveway and sidewalks. It won't be long until we're done."

In the afternoon, we did the same thing again at three different locations, although they weren't as big as the first one. After a day of riding the lawn mower and operating the weed eater, I didn't feel like I'd done any work at all.

When we got back to the landscaping business yard, Seth asked Dave, "How'd he do?"

"He's a keeper," replied Dave. "He didn't even come close to letting the lawn mower buck him off!"

"Good!" stated Dave. "Tomorrow he can clean up what me and the other boys left at the other job."

I had no idea what he and the other boys had left on their job, but I suspected it would be more work than what I had done today.

The next day we left the yard with different equipment. When we got to the job site, Seth explained to me, "This is a chipper. It makes sawdust out of tree limbs. We feed the limbs in here and the sawdust comes out here, into the trailer Dave is backing into position. Don't get your hands in here, it'll make hamburger out of them. Better put these on. It's required."

Seth handed me a hard hat, a face mask, and ear plugs. I put my cowboy hat in the truck and donned the required equipment.

Dave and I kept the chipper busy while Seth and the other hands loaded the larger limbs and tree parts on a trailer. When the trailer was loaded, one of the hands took it back to the yard to unload it. Another trailer was put into position and loaded.

When the second trailer was loaded, we took a break. Seth came over to me and explained, "The larger limbs and such, we'll cut up into firewood at the yard. That's what you'll be doing tomorrow, running the chainsaw and splitter."

At the end of the day, I felt like I'd done a long day of physical labor and used some muscles I didn't know I had. The next day I was more tired than I'd been the day before. I operated the splitter and there was a lot of bending over, putting fireplace-sized wood on the splitter and stacking the split wood.

That's the way it went for the next few weeks. I got to the point where I really looked forward to the lawn mowing days. Riding the lawn mower was really a lot easier than feeding the chipper and operating the splitter. We worked six days a week, taking Sundays off.

Finally, the time came when I had to leave and show up at the dude ranch for my winter riding job.

I got Seth alone and said, "I need to be leavin' for my ridin' job in three days, like I told you when I hired on."

"You sure you want to leave?" asked Seth.

"I need to," I replied. "I told 'em I'd be there and I think they're countin' on me."

"We could use you on a permanent basis, if you want," said Seth.

"I'm committed," I said.

"I'll have your check ready. Just when do you plan on leaving?"

"I can work for the next three days. If you don't mind, I'll stay the night of the third day and leave the next morning," I said.

"That'll be fine," replied Seth.

The morning of the fourth day, Seth was there with my check. As he handed it to me, he said, "If your winter job doesn't work out, you've got a job here if you want."

"I'll keep that in mind," I said.

Disappointment Then Trouble

I drove out of the yard and headed to my winter job. Before I left town, I cashed the check. It was a considerable amount of money and I put it in the jockey box of the car for safekeeping.

I drove to the dude ranch, looking forward to getting back in the saddle again. I was more comfortable with a riding job, around the horses and cattle. I'd felt a little out of place working for Seth and not really knowing what I was doing. That feeling went away after I'd spent some time on the job, but I was still uncomfortable.

I was surprised when I pulled into the dude ranch. There were no cars around, and although the place still looked well maintained, it was essentially deserted. I'd expected to see a lot of people around. There were a few horses in the corral, but not the number I'd expected.

I walked into the office and nobody was there. I went down to the barn and found Steve oiling a saddle.

"Howdy!" I said.

"And howdy back to you," replied Steve.

"Where is everybody?" I asked. "I expected to see a lot of people here for the beginning of the season."

"Well," said Steve, "I've got some bad news for you. The place has been sold. I'm the only one here, just feeding the horses and kinda looking after things."

"Sold!" I said, astounded. I didn't know what else to say.

"That's right," replied Steve. "It came kinda sudden. Nobody knew about it. Everyone was let go as soon as the sale was finalized. They kept me here just to look after things and keep the horses fed."

"I guess that means I don't have a job," I said, dumbfounded.

"That's right," replied Steve. "I would have called you, but

I didn't have a phone number where I could get a hold of you. I'm sorry."

I didn't know what to say. I thought about going back to work for Seth, but didn't want to spend the winter sleeping in my car.

"Any idea who bought the place?" I asked.

"Nope. The movie star owner just sold it. I think there was a lot of money involved. I don't know who bought it or what they're going to do with it. There's nothing I can do. I suppose I'll be looking for another job soon."

"Any idea who's hirin'?" I asked.

"There's a few other dude ranches around that might be hiring," answered Steve. "You might try them."

I got directions to the other dude ranches, shook hands with Steve and left, very disappointed. I didn't know what I was going to do, except look for another job.

I drove to the other dude ranches Steve told me about, talked to the bosses, filled out their applications, but without success. The people I talked to were all nice, but they'd already filled their winter positions. A few of the guys told me to call back periodically. They weren't sure how long some of the help were going to last.

Another night sleeping in the car didn't seem too appealing, so I got a motel room for the night. It felt good to stretch out on a bed rather than curling up on the bumpy old car seat.

The next morning, I was up early and went to the sale barn, hoping to find someone that might be looking for help. I checked in at the office and nobody knew of anybody who was looking for help offhand. As I was leaving the office, I was approached by an older man.

"I understand you're looking for work," he said.

"Yep," I answered, as I sized him up.

He was well dressed, clean jeans with a crease running down both legs. It looked like the crease had been sewed in rather than just pressed. His shirt was clean and looked to be heavily starched. His hat was clean, not showing any sweat stains, and his boots were shined, not showing any corral dust. He was too clean to be a regular cowboy. I figured him to be a ranch owner.

"Can you drive a two-ton truck?" he asked.

"Yep," I replied.

"I need some livestock hauled out to my place. A couple of loads of cattle and a load of horses. There's three days' work if you want it."

"When does this have to be done?" I asked.

"You can start tomorrow if you want. There might be four days' work depending on what I can get bought today," he answered. "You got a driver's license?"

"Yep," I replied. At this point, I had him figured to be a cattle buyer.

"Let's see it."

I pulled out my wallet and showed him my driver's license.

"Everything seems to be in order," he said, handing back my license. "Do you want the job?"

"What's it pay?"

He told me and I thought it was about twice what it should have been for a day laborer. But I didn't say anything and accepted the position.

"By the way," I said, "what's your name?"

"I'm Butch Wolfe. I've got a load of cows at this barn that needs to be hauled home. You want to start now?"

"Sure," I replied.

"My truck is the red Rio over there. The keys are in it. Back it up to the chute and I'll get the paperwork."

I noticed that the racks on the truck were newly painted. *Takes good care of his equipment,* I thought. I put the truck into position, opened the tailgate, and waited for him to show up. He showed up with the paperwork.

"Open the tailgate. The yard hands are bringing the cows now," he said.

"Tailgate's open," I said.

He gave me a look of surprise. "Good!" he said.

The cows came on the run and got on the truck. I was in position where I could close the tailgate when the last critter got on.

"Just where do I have to take these cows?" I asked, as I looked at the truck. It wasn't overloaded, weight wise, although we couldn't have got another cow on it.

"You've got about a three-hour drive to the place," he said. "Just stay on the main road. When you get to the sign that says Spring Wells Ranch, turn left. My place is at the end of the road. Unload the cattle and put them in the first empty corral. My man out there should have feed put out for them. Give him the papers. Then come back here. I'll be waiting for you."

"Right," I said.

I got in the truck and checked the gas gauge, it was full. I left, contented I was earning some money. I thought I'd sleep in the car again that night.

I drove for about two and a half hours, found the sign that read Spring Wells Ranch and turned. The road was fairly well maintained and I thought I'd made good time.

The hired man was at the loading chute when I pulled up. I backed the truck up to the chute.

"You're late," said the hired man.

"I came as fast as I could," I said. "There are some pretty steep hills and sharp turns on the road."

The hired man opened the tailgate. "You got the paperwork?"

"Yep," I said, going back to the cab to get it. "Here," I said, as I handed it to him.

He took the paperwork and without looking at it said, "The boss will be waiting for you when you get back."

I took that last comment as an invitation to leave and did just that.

On the way back, I didn't think about anything in particular, other than where I could find more permanent work, at least for the winter.

The boss was in the auction waiting for me. He'd bought a few more cows.

"Everything go all right?" he asked, as I sat down next to him.

"Yep."

He gave me some money and said, "Go fill the truck. There's a gas station down the road. Bring back a receipt and the change."

I went and filled the truck and brought back a receipt and change. He put the money and receipt in his pocket without looking at it.

"They'll be another load in the morning. What time can you be here?" he asked.

"Anytime you want to start," I replied.

"I'll be here at eight," he said.

"Fine," I said. "I'll be here. I'm sleepin' in the car."

He reached for his wallet and pulled out some money. He counted out some, gave it to me and said, "Here's your pay. We'll see you in the morning."

I checked in at the office to see if they'd heard of anyone needing some help. Their reply was negative. Then I asked, "Would it be okay if I parked my car here overnight and slept in it?"

"I suppose so," was the reply from the lady behind the counter. "Just don't park where it will be in the way. We have trucks coming in and out all night."

"Yes ma'am," I replied.

I parked the car in a far corner of the lot and went back to the sale barn to get something to eat. I ate and went into the auction just to watch. I always enjoyed the cattle sales and was content to watch.

The next morning, I was waiting by the truck to haul another load of cattle when Butch showed up. He was dressed in much the same manner as he was the day before.

"Good mornin', Butch," I said.

"Morning," said Butch. "That's Mister Wolfe!"

"Yes sir," I said, surprised at the formality.

"The cattle you're going to take to the ranch are in pen D-four. Put the truck in position and go get them."

I backed the truck up to the loading chute, opened the tailgate and found pen four-D. I brought the cattle up the alley and loaded them in the truck. I noticed that there were a few lame or crippled cows in the bunch.

"Take these to the same place you took the load yesterday. Here's the paperwork. Then return here. I'll meet you here in the morning."

"Yes sir, Mister Wolfe," I said.

I started the truck and pulled out of the yard. As I drove to the ranch, I considered Mister Wolfe and his apparent formality. I thought it strange, but didn't dwell on it. I thought his formality and fancy manner of dress was strange for a gyppo-cow buyer.

On this day, I made better time getting to Spring Wells Ranch. I was already somewhat familiar with the road. When I got to the ranch, there was another truck just pulling away from the loading chute. The truck passed me going out and I noticed that the driver didn't wave.

I backed the truck up to the chute. The hired man was coming up the alley, opening the gate where he wanted the cattle.

"Turn 'em loose," he said.

I opened the tailgate, unloaded the cattle and followed them to the pen.

"You got the papers?" the hired man asked.

"Yep," I said, reaching into my pocket. I gave him the papers.

"Mister Wolfe has another load for you tomorrow."

"Okay," I replied.

"Then," continued the hired man, "he has a special load for you tomorrow night if you want it."

"Good," I said.

I left the ranch and went back to the sale barn in town, content that I had perhaps a few more days work. It meant a little more money.

I found Mister Wolfe waiting at the sale barn. He pulled out some money and paid me a day's wages on the spot.

"I've got another load of cows for tomorrow," he said, "but they're out at a farmer's place. We'll need to go pick them up in the morning. We'll leave here about ten. You can follow me to the farmer's in the truck. When you get the cattle to the ranch, my hired man will have a load of seven horses for you to haul farther up north, if you want. It'll take you most of the night, but I'll pay you another day's wages for it."

"Sure," I said.

"My hired man at the ranch will have a map for you on where to deliver the horses. When you get done, come back here. We'll take a day off, then I'll have another load of cattle for you."

Mister Wolfe reached in his pocket, pulled out a roll of twenty-dollar bills and handed me some. "Here," he said, "this is the next day's wages and there's enough there to gas up the truck."

I took the money, pleased that he was paying me in advance.

The following day, I followed Mister Wolfe, in his Lincoln Continental, out to a farmer's place where we loaded the cows. It was about three o'clock before I left and I knew it would be after dark when I got to the Spring Wells Ranch.

It was well after dark when I got to the ranch. I unloaded the cattle and looked around for the hired man. It was pitch black and I couldn't see anything. Soon, I saw a light coming from the house. It was the hired man coming to the corrals, muttering something about, "It's a rotten time of night to be delivering cattle and hauling horses. Someday he'll be sorry for it!"

"What'll he be sorry for?" I asked.

The hired man was surprised. "He'll be sorry for, ah ... getting me out this late at night. It's a rotten time to be hauling livestock."

"I turned the cows loose in the alley," I said.

"The gate's open. I'll follow them down to the corral. The horses you're going to haul are in that holding pen next to the chute. You can get them loaded while I close the gate to the cow pen."

Without a light it was difficult to get the horses loaded, but I managed. The hired man showed up just as I was closing the tailgate.

"I got a map for you, but it's up at the house. I forgot to bring it. I'll go get it for you."

"I'll follow," I said.

"No need," said the hired man. "I'll bring it back to you."

"But it'll save you a trip back," I replied.

"Don't bother. I can get it."

The hired man left and I waited for him. "It's kinda strange," I said out loud to myself. "He's never invited me in for a cup of coffee or just to visit. I could sure use a cup of coffee."

He returned and showed me the map by the light of his flashlight.

"Go directly to this place," he said. "Don't stop along the way. These horses are supposed to meet up with another load and they don't want to wait for you."

"You got brand papers?" I asked

"Ah ... they went ahead with another load. You'll be all right."

"If you say so," I said. I should have known something was not right, not having any brand papers and hauling horses in the middle of the night, but I didn't think anything of it. I was just happy to have a job.

I followed the directions on the map. There wasn't much

traffic on the road and I enjoyed the drive. It was so dark, I couldn't tell what kind of country I was in, but I knew I wasn't in the mountains. Relatively flat, rolling country with some long, slightly uphill grades.

I got to the place where I was supposed to deliver the horses. It was all dark except for a night light over the loading chutes. I backed the truck up to the chute and went back to open the tailgate and unload the horses.

Before I got to the rear of the truck, a bright light flashed on and a voice said, "Hold it right there, Bud! Put your hands in the air and don't make any movements! This is the sheriff! You are covered!"

"What's goin' on?" I asked.

"Be quiet and do as you're told. Do you have any weapons on you?"

"Just a pocketknife," I answered.

"Where is it?"

"In this scabbard on my belt," I answered.

"Ted, you go frisk him. I'll keep him covered. You got transport papers on these horses?"

"No," I said.

"How come?"

"I was told they came ahead with another load," I answered.

I was patted down and Ted said, "He's clean. Just a pocketknife,"

"Cuff him! Read him his rights."

I felt a hand on my upright left arm and it was put behind my back. I felt the cold, hard steel of the handcuffs close on my left wrist. The procedure was copied with my right wrist. Then I was told something about being under arrest for stealing horses and possession of a stolen vehicle. I was told if I didn't have a lawyer, one would be appointed for me.

"What's going on here?" I asked.

"You are under arrest."

"What for?"

"We have reason to believe these horses are stolen and that you stole them. You also have a stolen truck."

"I'm only haulin' 'em for Mister Wolfe," I said.

"Butch Wolfe?"

"Yes sir," I answered.

"Hum … how long have you been working for him?"

"This is my third day," I replied.

"Ted, take him over to your patrol car and put him in the back. See if he's got a driver's license and call it in. See if he's got a record."

My wallet was taken from my rear right pocket. "He's got quite a wad of cash here," said Ted.

I was helped into the back seat of the patrol car.

Still wondering what was going on, I sat in the car. There wasn't anything else I could do. I listened as the officer, Ted, called in my license.

With the information from the call, Ted said, "Just stay here."

I thought that was funny. I was handcuffed in the back of a police car. How could I go anywhere and if I could, what would I do? I could hear the officers talking over by the truck I'd been driving, but couldn't make out what they were saying. Apparently, there were more than two sheriffs.

Presently, I heard the horses being unloaded from the truck. Ted returned to the car and started it.

"Where we goin?" I asked.

"Looks like you're going to spend some time in jail. You'll get to see the judge about ten this morning."

"What time is it now?" I asked.

"It's a little after three," replied the sheriff's deputy.

It took about an hour to get to town and I was booked into the county jail.

A Strange Twist of Events

After being booked into jail, I was placed in a cell. The hand-cuffs were taken off. My belt and boots had been taken from me. I paced in the jail cell for a time, decided there wasn't anything I could do at the present, and laid down on the cot and fell asleep. Before I went to sleep, I thought, ironically, that it was nice to be able to stretch out rather than sleep cramped up like I did in my car.

I slept well, considering I'd never been in jail before. And I slept well past my normal wake-up time. Around nine o'clock, I was awakened.

"You get to see the judge! Get up!" It was a different officer that woke me. I was given my boots, handcuffed, and escorted to the city hall. The judge, a woman, was already seated when we got to the courtroom.

I looked around the room and didn't see anybody that I recognized. There were some other cowboy-looking fellers in the courtroom, seated toward the front. I could tell they were cowboy types, they all had farmer tans on their faces. The lower parts of their faces were well tanned and their foreheads were pale. They looked much as I did.

I listened as the charges were read against the other cow-boy-looking fellers. I didn't know what was going on, but thought I had got mixed up with a ring of cattle thieves and horse rustlers.

Before my name was called, I saw Mister Wolfe enter the court accompanied by a sheriff's deputy. He was handcuffed and looked different than he had the previous times I'd seen him. His clothes were wrinkled, like he'd slept in them all night. I was relieved to see him, he was my employer and my way of getting out of this mess.

"Claxton, William Claxton."

My name was being called.

"Approach the bench."

I got up and walked to the bench, still handcuffed.

"Mister Claxton, you have been charged with being in possession of a stolen vehicle and horse stealing. How do you plead?"

I started to explain that I had been hired to drive the truck and haul livestock for Mister Wolfe, but was interrupted.

"How do you plead, Mister Claxton?"

Without thinking, I said, "Not guilty."

The judge said, "Mister Claxton, you were caught with a load of stolen horses in a stolen truck!"

"Yes ma'am. But there are extenuating circumstances," I replied.

"Very well," said the judge. "You will be bound and held in the county jail. Do you have a lawyer?"

"No," I replied. "I'm just passing through."

"Can you afford a lawyer?"

"No, ma'am."

"Very well," replied the judge. "One will be appointed for you. Trial will be held in one week on December third. Do you have bond money?"

"No," I replied.

I was escorted from the court by a sheriff's deputy. On the way back to jail, I thought it funny that I'd been looking for a job where I could spend the winter with room and board, but had ended up in jail. Room and board was taken care of, at least for the next week!

That afternoon I had a visitor. A woman. She was escorted to my cell by a deputy.

"I'm Nancy Short, your court-appointed lawyer," she said upon being locked in an adjoining cell. "Are you William Claxton?

"Yes ma'am. But most folks call me Will."

"Okay, Will. Do you want to tell me what's going on?"

I explained the situation to Miss Short and how I'd come to be in Mister Wolfe's employ. Then I said, "I saw Mister Wolfe in court this morning. What was he doing there?"

"He was being held on a horse-stealing charge."

"What happened to him?" I asked. "I haven't seen him in jail."

"He's been freed on bail," replied the lawyer.

The lady lawyer asked me a lot of questions like, "Where were the horses stolen from and when?" I didn't know the answer to most of the questions and told her so.

It was beginning to look like, to me anyways, that Mister Wolfe ran a very widespread ring of horse stealing covering more than one state.

After more questioning, Miss Short said, "Based on what you've told me, it looks like you're an innocent victim of circumstance rather than an accomplice in this matter."

"That's right," I said. "I only worked for Mister Wolfe for three days."

"Our job now is to convince the judge you were not an accomplice."

"Don't I get a jury trial?" I asked.

"You can get one if you wish, but it would be easier to convince one person of your innocence rather than twelve," said the lawyer.

"Whatever you say," I said, "you're the lawyer."

Miss Short made preparation to leave. "Tim!" She called the jailer.

"You know him?" I asked.

"Yes, he's my husband."

"That's strange," I said. "He keeps 'em an' you free 'em!"

Nancy Short smiled. "I suppose you could look at it that way. I'll be checking in on you occasionally before the trial."

"Feel free to do so," I said. "I'm not goin' anywhere."

The next week was very boring, except for an occasional visit from Missus Short. I did get to know her husband some. On one of her visits, she said, "When they arrested you, you had a sizeable amount of money on you. Where did you get it?"

I explained how I'd been working and camping out between jobs. I also said "Mister Wolfe paid me daily, in cash."

"No paper trail," said Missus Short. "Mister Wolfe has a trial a day before yours, you will be called to testify."

"I'll be glad to testify against him," I said. "He's the one that got me into this mess."

The day of Butch Wolfe's trial, I was taken to the court-house, in handcuffs. When asked by the prosecuting attorney what my relationship with Mister Wolfe was, I retold my story. When done, Mister Wolfe's attorney asked me if I had been driving the stolen truck.

I answered, "Yes."

"Where did you steal it from?" he asked.

"I didn't steal it," I said. "Mister Wolfe gave me the keys to it when I started to work for him. I didn't know it had been stolen."

The prosecuting attorney had no further questions, but the defense attorney did have one. On redirect, he asked, "Did you notice anything different or peculiar about the truck?"

"Yes, sir," I answered.

"What was it?"

"I noticed that the racks had been freshly painted," I answered.

"Did you think anything strange or unusual about this?" asked the lawyer.

"Nope," I answered. "I just thought Mister Wolfe took good care of his equipment."

There was a laugh from the others in the courtroom and I was dismissed, but allowed to stay in court in case I was called to testify again. I watched and listened as the trial progressed.

I recognized Mister Wolfe's hired man from the Spring Wells Ranch. I hadn't seen him in jail, but apparently he was being held. He was handcuffed.

When asked if he'd ever seen me, he looked at me and replied, "Yes. He delivered some cows to the ranch." I thought it was strange that he was being tried.

The testimony of the other cowboy-looking fellers in the courtroom was confusing and I couldn't tell who was telling the truth and who was not.

Finally, Butch Wolfe was called to testify in his own defense. When asked if he'd ever seen me, his reply was, "I've never seen him before in my entire life!"

I started to stand and call him a liar, but Missus Short stopped me. "You'll have your chance."

Before long, the trial of Butch Wolfe ended and the jury was sent into the jury room to arrive at their decision. They returned about two hours later. I was taken back to my jail cell and Missus Short came to tell me of their decision.

"Butch Wolfe and his hired man and their accomplices were found guilty of horse stealing and being involved with a stolen truck," said Missus Short.

"How long will they get?" I asked.

"I don't know. Sentencing will be in a month. They'll be in jail until then."

"Too bad they don't still hang horse thieves," I said.

"Your trial is tomorrow. We'll meet in the judge's chambers."

"What are my chances?" I asked.

"I feel very confident that we can convince the judge that you were an innocent victim in this case. We'll have the same judge that presided today."

"That's good," I said. "Maybe I can get out of here."

"Where will you go?" asked the lawyer.

"I don't know," I replied. "I was lookin' for work when Mister Wolfe hired me. I'll just keep lookin'."

"Be ready before nine," said Missus Short.

"I can't do anything but be ready," I replied.

The next morning, I was escorted to the judge's chamber by Mister and Missus Short. The judge was waiting, but not in her judge's robes. Tim Short took off the handcuffs. He kissed his wife and left the room.

"I hope you don't mind doing this informally," said the judge.

"No, ma'am," I said.

"I listened to your testimony with great interest yesterday at Butch Wolfe's trial," said the judge. "I almost thought that you were the only one telling the truth during the whole proceeding. Do you have anything to add to or change what you said yesterday?"

"No, ma'am," I answered.

"Missus Short," said the judge, "do you have anything to add?"

"Yes, your Honor," said the lady lawyer. "I move that the charges of horse stealing and possession of a stolen vehicle against my client, Mister William Claxton, be dismissed and that these charges be expunged from his record. He has no previous record and he has merely been an innocent victim of circumstance."

"I understand the situation," said the judge. "However, your client was in possession of a stolen vehicle. Even though there were extenuating circumstances, under the law I must find him guilty of that charge, even though it is a lesser charge, receiving stolen property. Therefore, I must sentence him to the minimum term in jail as prescribed by law. Mister Claxton, I sentence you to six months in the county jail for receiving stolen property. However, I will suspend that sentence and place you on probation on one condition, if you agree."

"And what is that condition, your Honor?" asked Missus Short.

"The condition is simple. Mister Claxon must agree to go to

work for the county and care for the stolen horses on the ranch where he was arrested. He must also get the names of persons and license numbers of any vehicles entering the property and turn them over to the sheriff as quickly as possible. There might be more to this situation than meets the eye. Can you do that, Mister Claxton?"

"Yes ma'am," I answered.

"You will be paid at the rate of the county maintenance workers and you must continue until your six months' probation is completed. In the meantime your attorney can work to have your record cleared. Do you agree?"

"Certainly," I said.

"Miss Short can take you to the probation office and you will need to adhere to their terms," said the judge. "Mister Claxton, you are free to go."

I thanked the judge, and my lawyer and I left the judge's chamber. On the way out, I asked Missus Short, "Just how much did you have to do with the decision today?"

"Not much, really. But the judge and I did meet for a time after the trial yesterday. She was concerned that the stolen horses might not be properly cared for and that there might be more horses showing up at the ranch. She thought you might be willing to do the job and when I told her you were looking for work, well, things just sort of worked out from there. I did tell you she was a horse lover."

"Well," I said, "I sure do appreciate it. I suppose I'll be a spy for the county if any more stolen horses show up. If there's anything I can do for you in the future, just let me know."

"Just stay out of trouble," said Missus Short.

I was taken to the probation office and given my instructions. "Just report in once a month, in person," I was told.

Nancy Short gave me a ride to the sale barn. I got in my car, went to the grocery store and got provisions, then drove to the ranch where I was arrested.

I went to feed what horses were in the corral, but someone had already fed them. The house needed some cleaning up, so I did that.

As I fixed supper that night at my new home, I thought it ironic that I had been arrested for horse stealing, went to jail for horse stealing, and ended up taking care of stolen horses and perhaps receiving more stolen horses.

I went to bed thinking I was lucky. I'd been looking for a job, went to jail and as a result, got a job. I was set until the spring.

A Spy?

The next morning I had breakfast then fed the horses. I looked the horses over very closely. There were a few pretty good-looking horses in the bunch, some had saddle marks on their withers. For the most part, the others were skinny and underfed. I couldn't see any brand marks on them and figured them to be mustangs. I thought they were destined for a slaughterhouse somewhere. I counted the horses and there were nineteen, including some yearlings.

Not having anything else to do, I got my saddle from the car and decided to ride around the ranch. There wasn't much hay in the stack yard and I thought if I could turn the horses out on pasture, the hay would last longer. I got a halter and entered the corral to catch a horse.

The horses I figured to be mustangs immediately ran to the far end of the corral when I went in. The better-looking horses just stood and watched me. I picked a bay-colored horse that had saddle marks on him, took him to a smaller corral, hobbled him and saddled him. I untracked the horse, and not knowing anything about him, cheeked him and stepped on him.

I was ready for the horse to become unglued and start bucking, but he didn't do anything. I rode him around in the small corral just to make sure he wasn't going to do anything. I was pleased that the horse responded to leg cues and neck reining. Satisfied that the horse wasn't going to do anything unexpectedly, I opened the gate and rode out into the pasture.

It was good to be in the saddle again. The week I'd spent in jail hadn't soured my riding skills. I thought it best to ride fence and make sure the horses couldn't escape if I turned them out. As I rode, I checked the feed conditions. There was some grass, not very much, but enough to lighten the pressure on the small stack of hay back at the ranch.

I did find a gate open at the far end of the pasture and I closed it. I noticed that there wasn't any water in the pasture, but decided to leave the gate open to the corrals, where horses could water.

Riding back to the ranch, I decided to keep the horse I was riding in the corral during the day and night and turn out the others. I would gather the horses each morning and corral them, perhaps give them a little hay. They could water in the corral each day. Bringing them into the corral would get them used to being gathered each day.

When I got back to the ranch, I turned the horses loose, unsaddled my horse and put him in a smaller pen.

I went through this procedure every day, gathering the horses each morning. The first morning, gathering was a little difficult, but as the horses became used to the procedure, the process became easier.

About the fourth or fifth day, I'd lost track of time, a truck showed up around eleven o'clock at night. The driver honked his horn when he entered the yard and it woke me up. I got dressed and grabbed a flashlight and went out to meet the truck.

As I approached the truck, the driver asked, "Where's Shorty?"

I didn't want to tell him that Shorty was in jail, so I said, "He's indisposed."

"Who are you and what are you doing here?" the driver asked. His voice was gruff and sounded somewhat annoyed.

"I'm Will Claxton. Mister Butch Wolfe hired me to fill in for Shorty while he's gone." It was a lie, but I didn't want to tell him that Wolfe and his crew were in jail and I was actually working for the county. "Who are you?"

"I'm just a driver delivering these horses for Mister Wolfe," replied the driver. "Where do you want them?"

"The gates are set, just turn 'em loose," I said. "How many you got?"

"There are seven," replied the driver.

The horses were unloaded and I followed them down to an empty pen and closed the gate behind them. I went back to the loading chute and asked the driver, "You want a cup of coffee? I got some up at the house an' it won't take long to heat it up. It's late an' a cup of coffee might help you."

"That sounds like a good idea," said the driver.

I pointed the flashlight at the truck, making a mental note of the license plate number and the make of the truck.

"That should be all right there," I said, trying to disguise my true actions.

We went to the house. I heated up the coffee and the driver sat down at the table.

"How long will Shorty be gone?" asked the driver.

"I don't know," I answered the driver.

"How long you been here?"

"About a week or so," I replied.

When the coffee was heated, I poured the driver a cup, poured one for myself, and sat at the table across from him.

I studied him closely. I guessed him to be about forty-five to fifty, average size with no distinguishing marks or features. His gruffness, displayed out by the loading chute, vanished as we talked. He appeared to be a fairly nice fellow.

As we talked, he opened up a little. As he loosened up, I asked him, "Who are you. I didn't catch your name."

"I'm Clark," he answered. "I'll be bringing another load of horses next Thursday, about the same time."

"What's today?" I asked. "I've sorta lost track of time since I've been here."

"Today's Sunday," answered Clark.

"Well, looks like I missed church," I said jokingly.

"Yep," replied Clark.

We finished the coffee and Clark got up to leave.

"I'll follow you to the truck," I said.

"That won't be necessary. I can find it," said Clark.

"But I've got the light," I said. "It'll be easier."

"Suit yourself," said Clark.

I led the way to the truck using the flashlight. I took a little longer way, making sure I got a good look at the license plate. I had the number memorized. I noticed that the front and rear license plates were from different states.

Clark got in the truck, started it and said, "See you Thursday."

"Sure," I answered.

After Clark left, I went to the house, wrote down the license numbers of each plate and the make of the truck and a description of Clark as best I could. Then, I called the sheriff's office and left a message for the sheriff to call me in the morning.

The next morning, I gathered horses as usual. When I finished, I went to the house, fixed breakfast and ate. After eating, I called the sheriff's office.

"This is Officer Tim Short," answered the voice on the other end of the line.

"Mister Short," I replied, "This is Will Claxton. I have some information for you."

"Where have you been? I've been trying to get a hold of you all morning. We had a message you'd called last night."

"I been doin' chores," I replied.

"What's the information?" asked Officer Short.

"I got a load of horses last night. I think they're stolen. There's another load coming Thursday night, about eleven."

"Do you have anything else?"

"Yep." I replied. I gave him the information I'd written down.

"I'll be out to see you this afternoon," said Officer Short. "We'll make some preparations to capture these horse thieves." He thanked me, told me to stay close to the ranch, and hung up.

Tim Short showed up around two in the afternoon. I showed

him the horses that had come in during the night. There were brands on a couple of the horses. Officer Short drew the brands in a notebook and said, "I'm not sure, but I think we got a notice of those branded horses being missing. I'll check it when I get back to the office. You say there's another load coming Thursday night, about eleven?"

"Yes sir," I replied. "That's the information I was given."

"We'll be here before then and get them! We'll show up early and tell you what to do."

"Okay," I said.

I maintained the same procedures during the week. Thursday, about noon, Tim showed up. I noticed that he wasn't dressed in his police uniform; he was dressed more like a cowboy. He did have a two-way radio on his belt and a revolver strapped to his side.

"We'll need to hide my car," he said. "You got a good place?"

"In the barn. It's the only place we can put it where it's out of sight. You the only one coming?" I asked.

"They'll be some other officers in the area later tonight. I can call them when we need them. You got anything to eat in the house?"

"There's plenty of canned stuff," I answered. "I ain't much of a cook from scratch."

"Anything will do," said Tim. "We've got a long wait until eleven."

We went to the house and visited. I learned a lot about Tim's early years. Growing up, he wanted to be a cowboy, but he got involved in law enforcement and decided to make a career of it.

Toward dark, I turned on the lights in the house. "Just to let him know I'm expecting him," I said. "I was sound asleep last time he came."

As eleven o'clock approached, I became increasingly nervous.

"Relax," said Tim. "Don't do anything to tip him off that we're here. Surprise is our biggest accomplice."

Around eleven, we heard a horn honk as it pulled into the yard.

"That's him!" I said.

"Just go out there like nothing happened or was going to happen. Act as natural as you can. I'll call Ted and have him show up in about fifteen minutes. Unload the horses and put them in a separate pen. Then invite the driver up for a cup of coffee. I'll be waiting for you."

I went down to the loading chute and greeted Clark. "Another load, huh?"

"Yep," answered Clark.

"The gates are set, turn 'em loose."

Clark opened the tailgate and we followed the horses to the empty pen. I closed the gate behind them and said, "Better come to the house. The coffee's hot already, I've been expectin' you."

"Sounds good to me," replied Clark. "Shorty never furnished any coffee."

I laughed to myself. I was about to furnish him room and board in the county jail.

We entered the house and when I closed the door, Tim stepped out from behind it with his gun drawn, and said, "Put your hands up! You're under arrest! I'm a sheriff's deputy."

Clark was taken totally by surprise. "Wha ... what's going on?" he stammered.

"We have reason to believe you're part of a horse stealing ring that's been operating in several states," said Tim as he handcuffed Clark.

Another car pulled into the yard and two sheriffs got out. They entered the house without knocking. I recognized the sheriff and Ted, the two officers that had arrested me.

"Hello, sheriff," I said.

"Everything under control here?" asked the sheriff.

"Under control," replied Tim. "I'll fish out his wallet and identify him."

The sheriff told Clark his rights, then he said, "You got anything to say?"

Clark just shook his head no and looked at me, disgustedly.

"Ted, put him in your car. We'll take him to jail."

When Ted and his prisoner left, the sheriff said to me, "Mister Claxton, you've done a good job for us. We do appreciate it. Tomorrow, Tim and the brand inspector will be out to identify the branded horses. They'll bring the people who reported the horses missing with them. You can release their horses to them with the brand inspector's approval."

"Yes sir," I answered.

"Tim, where's your car?" asked the sheriff.

"We put it in the barn. Didn't want anything to tip off the driver."

"Get it. I'll ride home with you. Mister Claxton, if you hear of anything else going on here, let us know. How many horses do you have here now?"

"With the seven that just came in, there are thirty-four," I said. "And if you get any information from Clark about more horses coming, let me know."

"Most assuredly!" replied the sheriff, "most assuredly!"

They left and I relaxed before going to bed. *This police work is interesting,* I thought, *but I wouldn't want to do it for a living.*

The next day, I corralled all the horses and kept them in. Around one o'clock the brand inspector and possible owners of the branded horses showed up pulling a gooseneck stock trailer. Tim followed them into the yard.

After introductions, the man and his wife were Mister and Missus Jennings, I took the people to the corrals and said, "The horses in question are in this pen." The Jennings entered the pen and immediately identified their horses. Mister Jennings went to the trailer and brought back two halters. He caught the horses and loaded them into the trailer.

When he returned, he got out his checkbook. "We've offered

a two-hundred dollar reward for the return of these horses. Who do I make the check out to?"

Tim said, "Make it out to Will Claxton. He's responsible for the return of the horses."

"But I can't take it," I said. "I was only doin' my job."

"You can take it," said Tim. "Technically, you're a private citizen. Take it."

Mister Jennings handed me the check and I thanked him.

"No," he said. "Thank you! These horses mean a lot to my wife and family."

Misses Jennings thanked me and gave me a big hug. I was totally embarrassed and could feel my neck becoming warm. I was blushing!

The brand inspector wrote out an inspection certificate for the Jennings and they left.

"I'd like to take a closer look at the rest of the horses," said the inspector.

"Sure. They're all there in the corral."

The inspector entered the corral and looked over each horse as best as he could. While he was doing this, Tim and I visited.

"My wife, Nancy, wants to know how you're doing out here," said Tim. "How are you?"

"You can tell her that I'm doin' just fine," I said.

"You don't mind being out here all alone?" asked Tim.

"Not at all," I said. "In fact, I've had more company the last two days than I've had since I've been here. If you don't mind, I'll stop in and see her myself when I have to visit my probation officer."

"Sure," said Tim. "I'm sure she'd like that. Her office is just across the street from the courthouse."

"Have you got any more information from Clark?" I asked.

"No. He's clammed up tighter than a drum. All he wants is his lawyer."

A Break in the Routine

The next few weeks went by slowly. My routine didn't change. I corralled the horses each day, fed them a little hay then let them loose. The brand inspector did show up one day to get a closer look at one of the horses, but nothing happened.

I told him, "I think those horses are broomtails. We ought to call the BLM and have them come and get them."

"I think you're right. I'll call them and see what they want to do with them. Is the sheriff holding them for evidence?"

"I don't know. But I'm runnin' short of feed. We can't have 'em starving to death at the hands of the county."

"I'll call the sheriff and look into it," said the inspector.

One night I got a phone call. It was from Tim Short.

"Will," said Tim, "my wife informs me that you haven't checked in with your probation officer this month. You need to come to town and do that tomorrow. If you don't, you'll have him looking for you! By the way, how was your Christmas?"

"I'll go to town tomorrow and take care of it. Has Christmas passed?"

"Yes," replied Tim. "It was two days ago. Didn't Santa Claus show up at the ranch?"

"Nope, I haven't had any visitors since the brand inspector showed up a week or so ago."

"No matter," said Tim. "You better come to town tomorrow."

The next day, I didn't gather the horses. They'd been coming in of their own accord to water each morning. But I did put out hay for them. I got cleaned up as best as I could and went to town. I checked in with the probation officer and everything was all right. The probation officer handed me a check drawn on the county.

"That's your wages for looking after the horses," he said.

"The judge had them send it to me as you don't have a mailing address. You'll need to come here to get your paycheck every two weeks. Of course, you won't miss our appointments." The probation officer grinned as he said that.

All I said was, "Yeah."

I took the check. The probation officer assured me everything was all right and I left. Then I went to the bank and cashed the check Mister Jennings had given me and the county check.

I then went to see Missus Short. She greeted me cordially and we had a nice visit. Before I left, I said, "We need to do something, either get more hay or get rid of the horses. We're runnin' short of hay and the feed in the pasture is gettin' scarce."

She also indicated that Judge McAdams was concerned about me.

"Judge McAdams? Who's that?"

"Judge McAdams is the judge who so kindly got you this job."

"Oh," I said. "Don't forget the hay."

"I'll look into it," said Missus Short.

With that, I went to the grocery store and got some supplies. Then I went to the feed store and got a sack of grain for the horse I'd been using. I was using him every day and even though I wasn't using him hard, I thought a little grain would help him out. Then I went back to the ranch.

One morning, a week or ten days after I'd gone to town, a semi load of hay arrived at the ranch. It looked like pretty good hay and my comment to Missus Short had paid off. The only thing wrong was that there was only the driver of the truck, one helper he'd brought, and myself to unload it. I didn't look forward to that job, but it had to be done.

I asked the driver, "Where did this come from?"

"The county bought it," he replied.

We spent the day unloading hay and stacking it in the barn. I didn't gather the horses, but they came in of their own accord.

They stayed in the corral for a while, watching us. I wondered if they appreciated our work. It was their meals we were storing.

It took us all day to unload the hay, but we weren't in a rush. The driver and his helper left and I resumed my routine. It was fairly boring, but it was a job for the winter and it sure beat spending time in jail. I went to town every two weeks or so to pick up my paycheck and check in with my probation officer. On these trips, I checked in with Missus Short. I thanked her for having the hay sent out.

Her reply was, "That was the work of the judge. She said we can't have these horses starving while in the custody of the county. Besides that, they are needed as possible evidence in the future."

I asked, "What happened to Butch Wolfe?"

"He's serving his time in prison. He got five years, if I remember correctly. However, it is believed he has a partner in another state and we're trying to track him down. All his accomplices have kept quiet, even with the promise of receiving lighter sentences."

On one of these visits with Missus Short, she said, "The BLM will be out next week to determine what horses are mustangs. They'll take those horses and do whatever they do with them."

"Won't the deputy sheriff need to be there when the BLM arrives?" I asked.

"No. The brand inspector will be there. According to the judge, you can release the horses that the inspector says are BLM horses."

"Very well," I replied. "What do you intend on doin' with the horses the BLM doesn't take?"

"We'll probably turn them over to a horse rescue operation. No one has stepped forward to claim them."

"You know, it's gettin' close to spring and the end of my probation. I'll be goin' up north to look for work when my term's over," I said.

"Yes," said Missus Short. "I think the judge will want to see you before you take off. I'm still working on trying to clear your record."

"I appreciate that," I said.

Until the BLM showed up, my routine stayed pretty much the same. When the BLM arrived with the brand inspector, I had the horses corralled.

The BLM man looked through the horses. It was fairly easy to pick out the wild horses—they all had long tails and scraggly manes. Of the thirty-two horses I had left, they took nineteen. They loaded them in the two gooseneck trailers they had and left. I had thirteen horses left, counting the one I was using.

Spring was approaching and the grass was starting to come up. I decided to keep the horses in and feed them every day. The new grass didn't have much feed value at this stage and I was afraid the horses would lose weight. Since the BLM took more than half of the horses I had, I thought I had plenty of feed.

On what turned out to be my next to last trip to town, my probation officer informed me, "Your probation is over. You won't need to see me anymore. But the judge wants to see you next week. You have an appointment with her next Tuesday at ten o'clock in the morning. Don't be late."

I returned to the ranch and continued my job of taking care of the horses. The following Monday, I loaded my gear and what canned goods I still had in the car and made ready to leave.

Tuesday morning I was up early. I put my bedroll in the car, gave the horse I'd been using an extra measure of grain and threw the other horses extra hay. I opened the gate so the horses could go out and graze if necessary. Then I went to town for my appointment with the judge.

I arrived on time and the judge and Missus Short were waiting for me in the judge's chamber. After greetings, the judge said, "Mister Claxton, you have successfully completed the terms of your probation and our agreement to have you care for the stolen horses. Your lawyer, Misses Short, has successfully petitioned the court to have your record cleared. Your record will show that you were arrested on suspicion of vehicular theft and horse stealing, but you were not convicted. The details have been omitted. Do you have any questions?"

"Does this mean I don't have to tell everybody that I'm a jailbird?" I asked.

"You are correct, sir," replied the judge. "You are free to go."

I thanked the judge, and Missus Short and I left the judge's chamber together. Outside, the lady lawyer asked me, "What will you do now, Will?"

"I guess I'll head north and look for work. I've pretty well missed the calvin' an' brandin' seasons. I don't know what I'll find. What will become of the horses left at the ranch?"

"The horses that are still there will be picked up by a horse rescue operation. After that, I don't know."

"And what will become of Butch Wolfe and his crowd?" I asked.

"Mister Wolfe and his cohorts are in prison and will be there for a considerable amount of time. However, they were only a small part of a larger operation covering a big area involving a few other western states. Our law enforcement officials will continue to try and track them down. If, in your travels, you hear of anything suspicious, let us know. We'd appreciate it."

"I certainly will," I replied. I thanked Missus Short and left.

I drove north, not knowing what I'd find in work. I was pleased that I was no longer a jailbird, but a little apprehensive about finding work. I regretted not being able to get in on the brandings, I loved heeling calves and dragging them up to a branding fire.

I drove north for a few days, camping alongside the road at night and occasionally getting a motel room so I could get a shower. The farther north I would go, the cooler it would be during the summer. I had plenty of money and wasn't too concerned about running short, unless I couldn't find a job. Then I might have to hire on with someone to help with the hay cutting.

As I got farther north, I began stopping at employment agencies to see if there were any riding jobs available. I didn't have much luck. I could have gotten a job if I wanted to irrigate or drive a tractor or swather in the hay fields. I was offered a job herding sheep, but I turned down these positions.

Back in the Saddle

I noticed the country changing as I went farther north. I was leaving the rocky, cactus country and getting into country that was more familiar. There were sagebrush and aspen. In the mountains, I entered pine tree country. I felt more comfortable.

I got into Nevada and at an employment agency, I heard about a job available packing salt. I checked into it. This late in the year, I thought it might be the only riding job available.

I got directions to the place and drove out to apply the next day. The road to the ranch went alongside a creek and there were cottonwood and aspen trees along the creek. Farther away from the creek was mostly sagebrush, but there was grass among the brush. This was the kind of country I was used to.

I got to the ranch headquarters and was pleasantly surprised. The main house was nestled among some cottonwood trees and there was a large lawn. The corrals were well organized and some distance from the house. The place was neat and clean and the outbuildings were well kept up.

I parked the car and walked to the main house and knocked on the door. I was about to knock again when it opened. I was greeted by a pleasant-looking woman who appeared to be about middle-aged.

Before she could say anything, I said, "I came about the job I was told you had available, packing salt."

"Yes," said the woman. "The agency called yesterday and said you were coming out today. I'm Sheila Brown. Come in. My husband, David, will be with you shortly. Can I offer you some iced tea or something to drink?"

"Some iced tea would be great," I said as I entered the house, taking off my hat as I entered. The house was clean and well kept. I was impressed.

As the woman left, David Brown entered. He extended his hand and said, "I'm David Brown."

I shook his hand and said, "I'm Will Claxton. I've come about the job opening you have."

"Sit down and tell me about yourself," said David. "Have you done any packing?"

"I've done a little packing, not much. I'm not really an experienced packer, but I can pack salt an' keep my horses from gettin' sored up," I said. I told him of my previous experience, leaving out the part about being locked up in jail.

"Well, that's good," said David. "But this isn't a straight riding job packing salt. There's fence that needs to be fixed and the bulls need to be scattered. There's the possibility of a few beaver dams that need to be opened up."

"I can do all of that," I said.

"I haven't been able to hire someone to do this. All the buckaroos don't want to get off their horse to do these chores. They think I should send out a fence fixing crew to do it."

"That don't bother me," I said.

"There's a line shack about forty miles from here where you'll stay. It's isolated and you'll be alone all summer," said David.

"That's fine," I said. "I sorta enjoy my own company."

David laughed. "Do you have your own saddle and equipment?"

"Yes," I said. "It's in the car. But I don't have any packin' equipment."

"Pack saddles, pack bags, and lash ropes are at the line shack, along with fencing equipment and some picks and shovels. Do you drink?" David asked.

"Nope," I replied.

"That's good," said David. "The last guy I hired to do this drank and spent all the time in the line shack, drinking."

We talked about wages and David said, "I can hire you if you want and you can follow me to the line shack in your car.

The road is a little rough, but you can make it if you take it easy."

"I'm ready now," I said.

"Then you're hired. We'll load some salt in my truck and get going."

We loaded about a ton of fifty-pound salt blocks on David's truck and started out. It took us about two and a half, maybe three hours to get to the line shack and when we arrived, David started honking his horn. I wondered why until I saw four horses come trotting into the corral. The honking horn was calling the horses.

I was immediately impressed with the appearance of the place. The line shack was set in a grove of aspen trees. There was a small barn and a round corral. There was a hand pump for water by the corral and an outhouse behind the shack. By the barn there was a small stack of hay.

Before we unloaded the salt, David closed to the corral then went to the small barn and got a nosebag of grain for each of the horses.

"This is their reward for coming in when they hear the horn," he said as we gave each horse his nosebag. "There's a small horse pasture here and there should be enough feed for the summer for them."

While the horses were eating their grain, David and I unloaded the salt. When we were done, we went back to the corral and took the nosebags off the horses. As we did this David explained a little about each horse to me.

"The two bays are broke to ride and they are pretty good horses. They'll give you all you ask for and you can pack either one of them. The black is only green broke, but you can pack him. You can ride him if you want, but be prepared. You'll never know what he's going to do. The paint is a packhorse and I don't think he's ever been rode. Use your own judgment with him."

I made a mental note of what David told me about the horses as we headed to the line shack.

"There's no electricity out here," said David. "There's some kerosene lamps, a wood burning stove you can cook on and it provides heat. Of course there's no phone. If you hurt yourself, you'll have to drive to the ranch to get help, or wait for me. I'll be up with supplies every week or ten days. I'll bring your meat in a box filled with dry ice. It should keep, if you cook up a lot of roasts. Occasionally I'll bring up some more hay. You'll want to keep in a horse to run in the others each day. If you grain them every morning when you run them in, they should pretty well come in on their own."

I was already familiar with the routine, as I'd used it when corralling the stolen horses earlier in the year, but didn't say anything.

"Tell me about the country an' where I'm supposed to take the salt," I said.

David sat down at the table and drew out a map of the country and where I was supposed to take the salt. "If I were you," he said, "I'd spend a day or two riding around the country, just to get my bearings. Then you'll know where to put the salt and see what fence needs to be repaired. Our border fence is thirty, thirty-five miles north."

"Good idea," I said.

After a few more instructions, David looked around the shack and said, "I'll be up in a few days with some more supplies. You should have enough to last until then."

He left and I was alone. I took my saddle from the car and started toward the barn with it, but decided I'd saddle a horse and ride around the horse pasture. There was enough daylight left that I could check the condition of the fence around the horse pasture.

I caught one of the bay horses, hobbled him and saddled him. When he was saddled, I took off the hobbles, untracked him, cheeked him and stepped up on him. In the saddle, I just sat there for a few seconds then touched him with a spur and asked him to move out. He walked forward without any hesitation. I turned him in both directions and he responded. Then I had him trot around the corral. He was well broke and I opened the gate and rode out to check the horse pasture. The other horses followed.

I rode around the horse pasture and didn't find anything wrong. I figured the pasture to be about two hundred acres and the feed was good. There were groves of aspens here and there and farther to the north there were pine trees.

I finished the circle around the horse pasture and rode back to the shack. I unsaddled the horse, but kept him in the corral and threw him some hay. I would use him to run in the other horses in the morning.

In the shack, I fixed up some supper consisting of canned stew. It was a lot better than the stew I'd had on the other outfit I'd worked on. After I ate, I went to the well and got water to wash the dishes and for coffee in the morning. I went to bed, content that I had a job but a little disappointed that I had to do my own cooking.

I hate doin' my own cookin', I thought to myself. Then I thought, *I don't mind doin' my own cookin', the part I hate is havin' to eat it!* I went to sleep, laughing at my own joke.

The next morning I got up, had some breakfast, caught up the bay horse, saddled him and ran in the horses. I grained them all and while the horses were eating, I saddled the other bay horse. I got to thinking that I need to name the horses, just to keep them straight. The bay horse I'd ridden yesterday had a stripe down his nose, so I called him Stripe. The bay I was going to ride today didn't have any markings, and he became Bay. The black was named Blackie and the paint became Spot. Not very original, but it would work.

When the horses finished eating their grain, I turned Stripe,

Blackie, and Spot out. I closed the gate, took the nosebag off Bay, took off the hobbles, untracked him and prepared to get on. From the way he was standing, I thought he might give me some problems, so I cheeked him, and swung into the saddle. I just sat there for a few seconds. I could feel the horse tense up as I sat in the saddle. Preparing myself for the worst, I touched him gingerly with a spur.

Bay took a big jump forward and to the right. I was ready and the horse didn't catch me by surprise. The horse hit the ground and stopped. I let him stand for a few seconds, then touched him with a spur again. He just walked out. I rode him around in the corral, turning him in both directions. I trotted him some. He was broke. I opened the gate and we rode out to do some exploring.

According to the map David had drawn for me, there was a creek off to the east and a number of salt grounds scattered around. I headed straight north at a trot and located a few areas where salt had been put in the past. They were located on the tops of hills or ridges and would help keep the cattle scattered.

As I rode, I noticed small bunches of cattle here and there. I rode through them and everything appeared to be all right. I saw that all the calves were branded, and regretted that I had missed out on the branding.

I rode about half a day to the north then turned east to circle back to the shack. I saw more cattle and found more salt licks. There wasn't any salt at the locations and I decided to pack salt the next day.

I made it to the shack before sundown, grained Bay and kept him in the corral for the night.

The next morning, I ran in the horses and grained them. I hobbled all the horses and put pack saddles on Blackie and Spot and put my saddle on Stripe. I turned Bay out. I'd used him pretty hard the day before and a day off wouldn't hurt him.

I loaded four blocks of salt on Blackie and four blocks on

Spot. Two hundred pounds apiece to carry would be just right for each horse. I took off the hobbles and put them in the pack bags. I tied a piece of baler twine to Spot's lead rope on the halter and tied it to Blackie's pack saddle. If Spot pulled back, the baler twine would break and none of the equipment would get busted up. I also tied baler twine around the sawbucks on the pack saddles to keep the pack bags on in case we had a wreck or started trotting on the way home.

I unhobbled Stripe, stepped on, grabbed up Blackie's lead rope and we headed out. I was doing what I was supposed to do. I passed the first few salt licks I came to, figuring on putting the salt farther out.

When I finally decided to throw out some salt, I got off my horse, hobbled him, then I hobbled the packhorses. I figured if the horses were all hobbled, I wouldn't lose any of them.

I unloaded Spot first. David had told me that the black was a younger horse and kind of unpredictable when someone rode him, so I thought the extra work might do him some good.

I threw off two blocks of salt at each location and started back toward the shack. On the way, I got to thinking. I had a ton of salt to start with. I could pack eight blocks at a time. That meant I only had five days of packing until I was out of salt. I decided I'd do some more exploring the next day. We'd covered a lot of miles this day, and a day's rest wouldn't hurt the horses.

On the way back, I came across a creek. I got out the map David had drawn for me and roughly located my position on the map. I was still a good way from the shack and glad that the days were longer. I figured I'd get back just about dark.

Upon reaching the shack, it was dark, I grained the horses and they ate as I unsaddled them. I kept Stripe in to run in the other horses the next day. I decided to ride to the west the next day and explore the country.

Early the next morning, I ran the horses in, grained them, and saddled Bay. When the three horses I wasn't going to use finished their grain, I turned them out so they could graze during the day.

I then stepped on Bay and we headed out at a trot to explore. We got some distance from the shack and the country became rougher. There were more rocks, it became a little steeper, and there were a lot of washes and gulches. There was a lot of sagebrush and quite a few piñon and cedar trees scattered around. Farther to the northwest, there were aspen trees and even farther, I could see pine trees. I found a few cattle, but not as many as on the east side, although the feed was just as good. I found some places where salt had been put out other years, mostly on the ridge tops.

I came across another creek and David hadn't marked it on the map. I got to wondering if I had strayed off the ranch property. I decided I'd only put out eight salt blocks on the west side until I was sure I was doing the right thing on the right property.

I rode farther to the northwest and the country became a lot rougher. I saw fewer cattle, but did notice some unshod horse tracks. I was a little surprised, as David hadn't mentioned anything about wild horses in the area.

I made a big circle in the western part of the range and it was well after dark when I got back to the shack. I grained Bay well as we'd covered about forty miles during the day, and kept him in to run in the horses the next day.

The next day, I saddled the two packhorses and Stripe and headed out to the west where I'd seen some salt grounds the day before. My routine became pretty much the same every day—run in the horses, grain them, then either pack salt or ride out and explore. I explored the west side more thoroughly than the east side and got to know it fairly well. I got into the pine trees I'd only seen from a distance before.

Coming out of a bunch of pines, Stripe suddenly became more alert. His ears were pointed forward. He nickered and

I saw some horses off in the distance. They'd spotted me and were leaving in a hurry. I did see a lighter-colored horse bringing up the rear. I couldn't really make out his color, either palomino or buckskin, he was too far away and the horses in front of him were stirring up some dust. *Probably the stud drivin' his mares away*, I thought.

I was fast running out of salt, I only had eight blocks left, and using the horses pretty hard. I decided to give them a day off and relax a little myself. I was sitting on the porch, drinking my third cup of coffee, thinking that if I had a few more packhorses and another saddle horse, I could take more salt each day. I was thinking this when a truck came driving up. I wasn't surprised to see David driving the truck.

He looked surprised to see me at the shack. "What are you doing here?" he asked.

"I'm about out of salt and the horses could use a rest," I said.

"Oh," said David, starting to walk toward the barn as if he didn't believe me. And that's what I thought as I followed him.

"You are about out," he said, looking in the barn. "In the past, the men we hired to do this still had half the salt they started with at this time. What have you been doing?"

"Every other day or so," I said," I'll pack eight blocks of salt out. The other days, I've been exploring. These cattle are really salt hungry. At some of the spots I've put out salt, it's already gone. Other places, it's half gone."

"I'll bring up a couple more ton in a day or two. I've got some groceries for you. You got any coffee left?"

"There's coffee in the house," I said as we started toward the house.

"You call this old shack a house?"

"Certainly," I said as I opened the door for him. "It's home. I live here! Come on in."

David laughed as he entered the house. I stoked up the fire in the stove. "I'll warm this up a little," I said.

David promptly turned around and started to leave. "I'll start bringing in your groceries," he said.

We brought in the groceries then David went back to the truck. I thought we'd brought in all the groceries. He returned holding something covered with a tablecloth.

"Sheila baked this for you yesterday when she found out I was coming up today. I had to keep it in front in the truck so as it wouldn't get mashed. He took off the tablecloth to reveal a pie.

"It's apple," he said.

"Well," I said, surprised, "if I'd have known you were comin', I'd have baked a cake!"

We sat at the table eating apple pie, drinking coffee and talking. David seemed pleased with what I'd done so far.

"I haven't been to the north boundary yet," I said. "I figure I've been coverin' about thirty-five or forty miles a day. To make it to the north boundary would be about a seventy or eighty mile day. That's kinda tough on horses, an' this is a big country."

"And tough on men," added David.

"Yep. But if I had another saddle horse an' a couple more packhorses, I could cover more ground. If I had a tent, I could make it up there an' camp at night."

"That's an idea," said David.

"An' while I was out that far, I could even move cattle farther north. Kinda kill two birds with one stone."

"I'll bring up a tent next time," said David. "I do have a couple more horses I can bring up. They'll both pack, but I'm a little short on saddle horses. Have you rode the black?"

"Nope," I replied. "I've just been usin' him for a packhorse. I figured I'd get him a little tired."

"He's been rode before, but he doesn't know much, and he's liable to come uncorked at any time."

"I'll try him sometime," I said. "By the way, I saw some wild horses over on the west side. They were on the other side of the creek you hadn't drawn on the map. There wasn't much water in the creek."

"I didn't draw it because I didn't think you'd get that far west and it usually dries up about the first of May. If you'd have gone three or four miles farther west, you'd have run into our west boundary fence. You say there's wild horses up there?"

"Yep. I saw 'em."

"Well," continued David, "That means the fence is down somewhere along the west side. The other side of the fence is BLM ground and there's a few wild horses on it. The BLM has tried to corral a yeller stud and his bunch, but the stud has always eluded them. They've even used helicopters. Have you made it to the old windmill?"

"Nope," I answered.

Mustangers

"There's an old windmill up there, I don't even know if it's still working. It should be, that's where the cattle water when the creek dries up. There's not many cattle over on the west side, even though the feed is pretty good. But we'd better find the hole in the fence and see if we can send the wild horses back where they belong. It's either that, or bring a rifle and put an end to them. If they're around when the creek dries up, they'll keep the cattle off the water."

"When the creek dries up, will the stud an' his bunch have to water at the windmill?" I asked.

"Yes, unless they return to the BLM ground."

"Well," I said, "we could build a trap. Keep 'em off water for a few days, then when they're good an' thirsty, let 'em in an' close the gate. They'd be captured then."

"That would probably work, unless the horses went back to the BLM ground."

"If they did that, we could follow 'em, then fix the fence where they went through."

"The trap idea would work," said David. "I'd need to bring up shovels, a chain saw, everything we needed to build a corral, including a gate and hinges. It would mean camping up there until the job was done."

"I could do that," I said. "When do you want to bring supplies?"

"I could bring salt and fence building equipment day after tomorrow," replied David.

"Good," I said. "You bring that stuff day after tomorrow an' I'll haul the rest of the salt tomorrow. We'll pack it up there the next day. I'll also need more grain for the horses. You might throw in some horseshoes and shoein' equipment. The horses shoes are gettin' a little thin." I felt a little guilty telling the boss what to do, but he seemed okay with it.

"There's an easier way," said David. "You're getting a little ahead of yourself. There's an old road through the BLM ground up to the windmill. I could haul the fence building equipment and a tent in the truck up to the windmill."

"Okay," I said. I could see where my limited knowledge of the country might prolong the operation. "Then I'll haul salt tomorrow an' help you unload salt the next day."

"The next day, when I leave, you come with me. Bring your bedroll and your saddle. You can stay overnight in the bunkhouse. We'll take the road around to the windmill along with a couple of ranch hands. It will only take a few days to build the trap."

"Why am I bringin' my saddle?" I asked.

"When we get this little project done, I'll give you another saddle horse. He isn't much, the ranch hands have been using him to irrigate with. I'll also give you two more packhorses. I like your idea about packing more salt every trip."

The plan was made. The next day, I hauled salt and the day after that, David brought me more salt. We unloaded the salt at my barn, I turned all my horses out, and I returned to the ranch with my bedroll and saddle. At David's suggestion, I took my dirty clothes and a change of clean clothes with me. David thought I might want to do laundry, which was a good idea.

The next day, we loaded the supplies we needed along with a large tent. David was bringing four ranch hands and someone to cook to help out on the project. When our supplies were loaded, David asked, "Do we need anything else?"

"Yes," I said. "We need a roll of smooth wire."

"Smooth wire?" asked one of the ranch hands. "What for?"

"When the trap is built, one of us will be hidin' behind a tree or some brush. When all the wild horses are in the trap, whoever's hidin' will pull the wire an' close the gate. Then we'll have the horses captured."

"How do you know it will work? Have you done this before?"

"I've never done it," I said. "But I've listened to old timers when they were talkin' about catchin' wild horses. We'll find out."

We got the smooth wire. We had everything loaded in two trucks and headed out. We took the long way and came to the windmill through the BLM ground. At my suggestion, we made camp about half a mile from the windmill. Perhaps the mustangs wouldn't be scared off by our camp if we set it up some distance from their watering hole.

David and I left the other hands and cook to set up camp and we took the truck and shovels to the windmill to look things over.

"They've been watering here occasionally," said David. "There are some unshod horse tracks around, but they're old."

"That's good," I said. "Our efforts might prove successful."

We unloaded the corral building materials and mapped out how we wanted to build our trap. There were plenty of cedar trees close by and we could cut them and use them for posts. We'd have to go farther up on the mountain to cut poles to complete the pen.

Looking the area over, I decided a good hiding place would be behind a large clump of chokecherry bushes. I needed to make sure we could close the gate with the wire attached to it and I needed to make sure the gate would stay closed when we pulled the wire after the horses were in the trap.

The next day, we were up early. David and one of the hands took the chainsaw and went to cut cedar posts. The rest of us started digging postholes.

I'd measured off the distance between each spot where a post was to be planted and figured it to be about twelve feet. If the poles were stout enough, it should hold the horses. I thought a three-rail corral should hold the horses, if it were built high enough. The trap would be about fifty feet long and about fifty feet wide. I figured it would hold the stud and his band of eight or ten mares.

David and the other hand returned with a load of cedar posts. They were all limbed and ready to go in the ground. We'd finished digging the postholes and were relaxing when they showed up. We put a post in each hole and David decided to call it a day.

"You can plant them tomorrow while I go get poles. It'll take me most of the day. I'll take another man, we might speed up the process if we're using two chainsaws. Will, you stay here and supervise the operation. When you get the posts planted, gather up some brush and limbs that we can stick in the fence. We want to hide it as much as possible."

The next day we did as we were told. When David got back to the windmill late in the afternoon with a load of poles, the posts were set and the rest of us were gathering up tall brush and limbs that we could hide the trap with.

I'd hung the gate from a stout cedar post and hung it just a little crooked so it would close against another post and the horses couldn't push it open. I propped the gate open with a stick. It was done so that if one of the mustangs knocked the stick over, the gate would still close. I strung the smooth wire from the gate through the chokecherry bushes, and tied a stout cedar branch to it. Then I pulled the gate shut a couple of times, just to test it out. It worked.

The following day, we nailed poles to the posts and wired the brush to the poles. When we were done, David said, "That looks pretty natural. Do you think it will fool the horses?"

"I hope it does," I said. "If it don't, we've wasted a lot of time and work makin' it."

"Time will tell," said David. "Let's go back to camp and start packing up."

"If we leave the tent an' cook stove an' groceries," I said, "I can use it when I'm packin' salt this way. It'll save a day or two."

"Good idea," said David. "We'll leave this setup alone until the creek dries up then come up and capture the horses. Wire the gate open. Hopefully, the horses will water here often enough that they'll be used to going inside before we come to capture them."

"That's the plan," I said.

We went back to camp. The other hands gathered up their stuff, mostly just bedrolls, and loaded it in the trucks. I put my bedroll in a truck and rode back with David.

Going back to the ranch, I said, "I really hope this works. I'd hate for you to blame me if it don't."

"Don't worry about that," he said. "You never know if something's going to work until you try it. Besides that, you'll have a place to keep your horses while you're camped here. You need to ride the fence on the west side and fix it where the stud came through. You can bring up the fencing tools on a packhorse. I'll bring up a ton of salt and some hay and leave it so you won't have to pack it so far. You might just as well stay at the ranch tonight. You can ride a horse and lead the two packhorses back to your camp tomorrow. While you're riding up here, I'll haul salt and hay to the windmill."

"Better haul plenty of hay," I said. "If the mustangs or cattle find it, it'll be gone in no time."

"I've already thought of that," he said. "I'll leave it on the truck, covered. That should discourage any horses or cattle from stealing our hay."

"You're way ahead of me on this deal," I said.

"We'll give the creek a couple of weeks to dry up, then I'll come up here, close the gate and we'll be set to capture some horses."

"You need to come an' get me for the capture," I said.

"I want to be in on the finish, seein' as I'm the planner in this operation!"

"You mean architect," said David.

"Yeah, that's what I mean, but I'm not sure I could pronounce it!"

I spent the night at the ranch and the next morning put my saddle on a sorrel horse David pointed out to me. David put a pack saddle on a paint horse. Then we put a saddle on a buckskin horse. I put my bedroll on the buckskin and tied it on with one of the lash ropes in a pack bag.

I untracked the sorrel and stepped on. Nothing happened, but I didn't expect anything. David had told me the horse was gentle, as were the two packhorses. He tied the paint's lead rope to the buckskin's tail and handed me the lead rope to the buckskin.

"I generally tie a piece of baler twine to the lead rope then tie the twine to the pack saddle," I said. "That way, if somethin' happens, nothin' will break, includin' the horse's tail."

"Nothing will happen," stated David. "These old boys have been led around like this for years. I'll check the condition of the creek in a few days. When it's dried up, I'll go to the windmill, close the gate then come up and get you. We'll capture that stud and his bunch."

"Come up in the evening," I said. "I'll be pretty busy during the day."

I started out for my base camp. On the way, I got to thinking that I'd sure miss someone else doin' the cookin. The man David brought to the windmill camp to cook did an excellent job. What he fixed was a lot better than anything I'd fixed.

I got to my base camp early in the afternoon, unsaddled the horses, put my bedroll in the house and turned the paint and buckskin loose. I'd use the sorrel to run in the horses in the morning.

I relaxed the rest of the afternoon and fixed myself a disappointing supper, after what I'd been used to eating. I got to wishing I'd signed up for and taken some homemaking classes with the girls in high school. I lamented this fact for a while, but didn't dwell on it. My poor cooking skills were already there and there wasn't much I could do about it. I decided I'd buy a small cookbook next time I went to town.

Early the next morning, I ran in the horses. I saddled the four packhorses and put my saddle on Stripe while they were eating their grain. I loaded four salt blocks on each packhorse, tied their lead ropes to the pack saddle on the horse in front of them, took the lead rope of the first packhorse and stepped on Stripe.

Without thinking, I touched Stripe with a spur and he took a big jump to the right. I was unprepared and almost fell off, but managed to stay on. I let the lead rope to the string of packhorses go when they pulled back from Stripe as he made his jump.

"That few day's rest has done you more good than I thought," I told the horse. I rode him around in the corral for a few minutes and satisfied that the kinks were worn out, grabbed the loose lead rope and started out.

I packed salt to the northeast, wanting to stay away from the windmill and not disturb the mustangs and put in a pretty long day. It was well after dark when I returned to my camp. I unsaddled the horses, grained them and turned them all out, except Stripe.

I went to the house, fixed myself some supper and thought, *I'd better start fixin' myself something to eat for dinner before I go out.* I hadn't eaten since breakfast and that was before sunup.

The next day, I saddled Bay and followed the same routine as the day before, except I put my bedroll on the buckskin and some groceries and a pot, knife, fork and spoon in the pack bags. As an afterthought, I put some grain and nosebags in the pack bags on the buckskin. I only had twelve salt blocks, but thought I'd ride all the way to the north border fence. I thought I might be gone a couple of days and wanted to be prepared.

I started out and didn't throw out any salt until I was well past where I'd thrown out the last of the salt I'd hauled the day before. I made it to the north border fence and still had six salt blocks left.

I camped by a spring that I thought fed the creek on the east side and slept out under the stars that night. I'd hobbled all the horses and hoped they wouldn't wander far. I'd grained them with the thought that the grain would keep them close to camp.

I went to sleep listening to coyotes howl.

The next day, I was up early. My horses hadn't wandered far and they were easy to catch with the grain. I caught each horse, unhobbled him, led him back to camp, rehobbled him and saddled him. I caught Bay first, I wanted to make sure I had a ride home.

I packed the remaining salt, my bedroll and groceries and started out again. I followed the border fence around to the southeast and soon had all the salt put out. I continued along the border fence, checking it as I rode. It was in good shape.

I made another open camp that night alongside the creek. I figured I'd be back to camp the next afternoon. A day off for the horses would do them some good and I could reset the shoes on them.

When I got back to camp, I unsaddled them, grained them and turned them all out, except Bay. I relaxed the rest of the afternoon. I didn't know how many miles I'd covered the previous two days, but knew it was quite a few. I was tired and so were the horses.

The next day, I got the horses in and started pulling shoes and replacing them with new ones. I really didn't like shoeing horses and didn't consider myself to be a good horseshoer, but it had to be done.

I took my time shoeing the horses and was halfway done with the second one when David showed up in the afternoon.

"The creek is dried up," he said. "We haven't had any rain and it's dried up early this year. We can go capture the wild horses."

"You seem pretty confident this plan will work," I said. I still had my doubts.

"Certainly it will," replied David. "Always think positive. Tomorrow I'll go to the windmill and close the gate. The next day, I'll come and get you and we'll get the mustangs!"

"I'll be ready," I said.

"Be sure and bring your bedroll. We might have to spend a few days."

"Yep," I replied.

The next day, about mid-afternoon, David showed up.

"You ready to go get some mustangs?" he asked. "There are fresh horse tracks around and in our trap. I closed the gate and tomorrow they should be plenty thirsty.

"Good!" I answered.

We loaded my bedroll, went back to the ranch and drove to the windmill through the BLM ground.

We camped that night where we'd left the tent. We inspected the trap and found everything to be in order.

"I don't know when the horses are watering," said David. "It might be early in the morning, might be during the heat of the day or along toward evening. We'll need to be hidden all day to make this work."

"It'll be boring," I said, "but I'm ready."

Early the next morning before sunup we were up eating breakfast. We went to the trap, I propped the gate open and we settled down behind the chokecherry bushes to wait for the horses to come in to water.

We watched the sun come up and noted the changing shadows as the sun rose in the east. I'd seen this many times before and always appreciated it. To me, sunrise always signified new life.

We stayed hidden all morning. Just about when I was ready to take a midmorning nap, David nudged me. "They're coming!" he whispered excitedly. "Don't move!"

The mustangs approached the trap warily, even though they hadn't had water for two days. The lead mare was very cautious, even though she'd been in the trap before. Hesitantly, she entered the trap and the other horses followed her. There were seven mares, four colts, and the palomino stud.

"They're all in," whispered David. "Pull your gate shut!"

I grabbed the stick I'd wired and gave it a good hard tug. The gate closed with a bang. The noise startled the horses and they began running around the trap.

"We've got them!" shouted David. "We've got them!"

The horses became more agitated as David got up, yelling. I didn't say anything. Although I'd had my doubts, I didn't want to appear overly excited, but it was all I could do to keep from jumping up and down like a little kid at Christmas, I was so excited. I walked up to the gate and wired it shut. The horses ran to the far side of the trap and nervously watched me.

David was happily slapping me on the back, saying, "You're plan worked! It worked!"

"We got 'em," I said as passively as I could. I tried to act like this is what I'd expected and had done it a thousand times before, although I hadn't. Inside I was secretly very pleased. "Now, what are we goin' to do with 'em?"

"We'll throw them a little hay, I'll take you back to your camp then call the BLM and tell them we've got some of their horses up here. Then they can do whatever they want with them."

"When you call 'em, better tell 'em to bring some panels so they can make a chute to load the horses," I said.

"Good idea," replied David.

We did as David outlined and left. When he took me to my base camp, I told him, "I'll be movin' up to the windmill tomorrow an' start ridin' fence the next day."

"You don't let any grass grow under your feet, do you?" stated David.

"Nope," I said. "If there's a job to be done, I'd just as soon get it done. When I've got the fence repaired, I'll start movin' some cattle over this direction. There's a lot of feed here that ain't bein' used an' there's no reason why it shouldn't be."

"That's a good idea," said David. "I'll be bringing you up more supplies in a few days."

David took me back to my camp and after he left, I started making preparations to move to the tent by the windmill.

Early the next morning, I ran in all the horses, saddled them, loaded my bedroll, groceries and fencing supplies and started toward the windmill. I had a string of seven horses to take with me, although some of the horses were carrying empty pack saddles.

I got to the trap in the afternoon, just as the BLM guys were loading the wild horses. I visited with them for a while before they left with the mustangs. Then I unsaddled all the horses and kept them in the corral that night.

The next day, after I turned the horses loose, all of them hobbled, I set out to do some exploring. This was all new country to me and I needed to find out a little about it. And I needed to find out where the fence was down. If the mustang stud had broken through it, it was very unlikely that the mares would have followed.

I rode the sorrel to the west, mainly trying to locate the west fence. I found it about an hour and a half later and followed it to the north. I found where the fence was down about two miles from where I'd found the fence. It hadn't been broken through, it looked like it was down due to heavy snowdrifts.

I looked over the situation and decided that I would need to rebuild the entire length of fence where it was down. I would wait to start the project until I'd talked to David. I'd like to rebuild the fence using steel posts rather than having to cut cedar posts and dig postholes.

Horse Breaker

I continued to explore the country on the west side the next couple of days. It was a tougher country—steeper hills, more rocks and denser brush. There was a lot of good feed in the area if I could move cattle in on it. They could water at the horse trap.

When David showed up a few days later, I told him of my plans to rebuild the fence.

"Do you want some help"? he asked.

"Nope," I said. "I can handle it by myself. I can fix the fence in three or four days with some steel posts and a steel post driver. Then I can push some cattle over this way."

"Buckaroos won't get off their horses to do that sort of thing," said David.

"I know. But I didn't hire on to buckaroo. I hired on to pack salt, fix fence, and move some cows around. So that's what I'll do."

"You're kinda unique," said David. "Most cowboys only want to cowboy."

"It all comes with the territory," I said.

"I'll bring up some steel posts and a driver tomorrow," said David. "By the way, do you want a paycheck?"

"A paycheck would be fine," I said. "But what would I do with it? Better keep it until fall when I leave."

"You'll stay and help us gather cattle in the fall, won't you?"

"I figured on it," I said.

"How many steel posts do you figure you'll need?"

"Probably about twenty," I replied.

"I'll have them here tomorrow. I'll also bring some clips. Stick around until I show up."

True to his word, David showed up the next day with

steel posts, a driver and a new roll of barbed wire. I was set to fix fence.

The next day, I packed the fencing supplies out to where the fence was down. I rode directly to it and made good time. I unloaded the steel posts, driver, and wire. I also had a fence stretcher and fencing pliers. When I had all the posts I needed driven in the ground, I decided to call it a day. I could stretch wire tomorrow and the fence rebuild would be done.

I looked forward to the next day. I didn't really like building fence, but it had to be done. The sooner it was over, the better.

The next day, I finished the fence. Satisfied that it was complete, I left, planning on coming back the next day with a pack-horse and bringing the fencing equipment back to camp. Then I could start moving some cattle around.

The summer passed on. I packed salt all over the range, continually checked fence and spent a fairly easy summer. The only real excitement I had was when I decided to ride the black horse one day.

I saddled him in the horse trap and he was calm. I'd been packing him all summer and he was used to being saddled. But after I untracked him and started to put my foot in the stirrup, he pulled away. I cheeked him more strongly and managed to get on. I sat in the saddle for a few moments, shifting my weight back and forth in the saddle. The horse didn't do anything.

When I decided to touch him with a spur, he came unglued and started bucking and bucking hard. The black could buck hard and he was doing his best. I was doing my best to stay on, but had to pull leather with my free hand. This wasn't a place to do any fancy riding. It was important to stay on!

I didn't do a fancy job of riding the black, but managed to stay on, just barely. When I finally got his head pulled up and he stopped bucking, I was really relieved. If he'd have taken one more jump, he'd have thrown me off. He was breathing heavily, but I didn't give him a chance to get his breath, I touched him with a spur again and he moved out. I urged him into a trot and kept him at it. While he was still winded, I pushed him into a lope around the trap. He made a minor effort to buck, but I kept his head up so he couldn't start bucking. When I figured he was good and tired, I stopped him and got off.

I led him around the corral on foot then got on again. He only half-heartedly attempted to buck. I rode him around inside the corral for about an hour, trying to teach him to stop and turn. David was right when he told me the horse didn't know much.

I decided I'd spend some time teaching him during the summer. But I'd do a lot of riding in the corral to do it. As my salt supply dwindled, I was able to spend more time riding the black. Slowly, but surely, he was learning, but was difficult to get on. I spent a long time getting on and off the horse and he finally settled down to some extent. I still cheeked him every time I got on. I didn't trust him one hundred percent. I thought that he'd probably been mistreated in the past and would need some time and lot of work to overcome it. But, he was getting better each time I rode him.

Moving cattle around to the west, and running the horses into the trap in the mornings, I used Stripe, Bay, or the sorrel. I kept the horses in the trap during the day and turned all but one loose at night.

The summer was wearing on. The days were becoming shorter and cooler. David had been bringing me supplies every ten days or so, but my time was getting short. It wouldn't be long before I needed to make ready for the fall gather, then go south, where it would be warmer for the winter.

Anticipating the fall gather, I started pushing cattle from the western range over to the eastern parts. These were mostly the same cattle I'd moved west earlier in the year. It would be easier to gather cattle on the eastern range than on the rough, tough western range.

One day, when David showed up, he asked, "Are you ready to start the fall gather?"

I'd moved back to my line shack by this time. "Yes," I answered. "I've already started pushin' cattle east. I figured they'd be easier to gather on the east side."

"That's good. The cattle generally come in on their own from the west," he said.

"You mean I started too early?" I asked. "I've moved a lot of cattle that way an' the feed was gettin' a little short."

"No," said David, laughing. "It's not too early. I was going to have you start. But since you've already started, you can bring your horses and your stuff back to the main ranch. We'll truck the horses to the windmill through the BLM ground and start our gather next week. I thought you'd like to go to town for a few days."

"I don't really have any business in town," I said. "However, I could use some new clothes."

"You take a few days and go get them. I'll have some money for you when you're ready to go."

"You mean I'm done?" I asked.

"No," said David, laughing again. "We need you to help bring all the cattle home. You've got a few weeks work left. You can stay and feed cows all winter, if you want."

"I'm not too interested in feedin' cows all winter." I said. "I'd like to go south an' find work where it's warmer for the winter."

"You can always find work here," said David. "You've done a good job here, better than I expected and better than anyone else I'd hired to do what you've done. Yes, you can always work here!"

"I appreciate that, but I'd rather move farther south," I said. "How many hands you got to help gather cattle?"

"Well," answered David, "They'll be Sheila, myself and you. None of the other ranch hands are really cowboys or horsemen. They're irrigators and tractor drivers."

I was surprised to find out that I was the only cowboy David had.

"We had one of the men help out gathering cattle one year," continued David, "But he gave out about mid-day and started walking in on foot. I had to go back and get him in the truck after we moved the cattle into a small holding pasture. He vowed he'd never get on a horse again as long as he lived." David smiled as he made that last comment.

"I'll help until we get all the cows home," I said.

"That's good enough for me," said David. "Tomorrow I'll go up to the windmill with Sheila and bring the truck and tent home."

The next day, I ran in all the horses, saddled them, loaded my stuff and what groceries I had left over and rode to the home ranch. I unsaddled the horses, and David took the groceries to the house. I put the pack saddles where they belonged and put my bedroll in the bunkhouse. I'd go to town tomorrow to get some new clothes.

I found it difficult to move into the bunkhouse. I was used to living alone and didn't involve myself in conversation with the other hands.

The next morning, after breakfast, I went to my car to go to town. David followed me, a grin on his face. I went to start the car and it wouldn't even turn over.

David laughed. "I thought so," he said. "Your battery's dead. I'll get the truck and give you a jump." He brought the truck over and we started my car. We let it run a little, just to charge up the battery

At David's advice, I refused to give any of the other hands a ride to town. "They'll likely get drunk, maybe land in jail and not be available for work. We still need them."

I was going to town alone, but it didn't bother me. I was used to being alone, even in a crowd. When I put my bedding in the car, David asked, "Are you leaving?"

"No," I replied. "I'm just goin' to do laundry."

"But you can do that here."

"I'll probably need four or five washin" machines an' four or five dryers. I can do a few months worth of laundry all at once.

"Suit yourself," said David. "You don't need to be back for a couple of days. Relax and enjoy yourself."

"I'll be back tonight," I said. "Probably late," I added.

"Well, here's your check. You can cash it at the bank."

I took the check and put it in my pocket without looking at it. I could get into town, cash the check, get some new clothes, do the laundry and still get back to the ranch before midnight. That suited me just fine, and that's just what I did.

The next morning, the farm hands waking up woke me up. I'd got in late and hoped to catch a little more sleep, but that wasn't possible. I showed up for breakfast and David looked surprised.

"I didn't expect to see you for a couple of days," he said.

"I'm here now," I said. I almost said that I end up in jail if I spend a lot of time in town, but didn't say anything.

"You just take it easy. We won't start gathering cattle for another couple of days."

"Okay. Where have you put my horses?"

"They're in a small pasture just south of the barn. They'll probably be in soon looking for grain. Why do you ask?"

"Just curious," I said. I planned on catching Blackie, riding him around some in the corral, then going outside on him. I'd never rode him outside the corral. The way he bucked the first time I tried him, I was leery of taking him outside the corral for fear he'd buck me off. I was worried I might get hurt or have a long walk home. Around the ranch, there was help to catch him if he got away or if I got hurt.

The horses came in looking for grain, and I grained every one of them then caught Blackie and saddled him. I'd just got on when David showed up.

"You decided to try him, huh?"

"Yep," I replied. "Blackie here don't know much, an' he's a slow learner, but he's coming along. He sure can buck!"

"You call him Blackie, huh? I call him Buster. He bucked me off two years ago and broke my leg. You're right, he sure can buck."

"I've never rode him outside the corral before. I figured I'd do it here where if he bucked me off, I'd have some help catchin' him up."

"Hold on a minute," said David. "I'll catch a horse and go with you."

David caught his saddle horse, a good-looking sorrel, saddled him and joined me. As we rode, we talked. David informed me that we'd gather the cattle, sort off the calves, then move the cows across the highway where they'd winter on hay fields. He informed me that it should take four or five days. He'd keep the calves in and have the farm help throw them some hay. He'd consigned his calf crop to a cattle buyer earlier in the year and was expecting a good check. He'd call the cattle buyer when we had all the calves and the buyer's men would come and haul them to a feed yard.

"Aren't you goin' to keep any replacements?" I asked.

"Nope. We culled pretty heavy last year and kept back more heifers than we needed," said David. "I was thinking we'd overstocked our range, but you kept the cattle scattered pretty good. It looks like we lucked out."

Riding Blackie outside the corral was good for the horse. I'd taught him to turn each direction and taught him to stop. With more riding, I thought he'd turn out to be a pretty good horse. I didn't have any trouble with him the rest of the day.

A few days later, we started the fall gather. I decided to use Blackie the first day thinking the first day would be the toughest. We trucked the horses up to the windmill in a two-ton truck. It was just Sheila, David, and myself. David and

Sheila were riding good-looking horses. I had some misgivings about how successful our gather would be with just the three of us.

When I stepped on Blackie, he bucked a little, it was more like a crow hop, but I pulled his head up and he stopped. Sheila looked a little surprised at Blackie's action, as she'd been told Blackie was about broke.

We started toward the east fence. David dropped me off first. I was to push any cattle I found to the east. David would pick them up along with the cattle he found and push them farther east to Sheila. Sheila would move all the cattle along the east fence until she got to the corner where she would hold them until David and I showed up. David would count the cattle through the gate.

I'd thought that David had given Sheila the big circle to ride but found out later that I had the biggest part of the riding to do. I was glad that I'd started pushing cattle from the western part of the range toward the east before I left the main camp. It certainly made the gather easier, even though Blackie and I covered a lot of miles that day. It was push cattle east until I saw David, then go back to the west and push more cattle toward the east.

By the end of the day, we'd gathered almost all of the cattle. It was a fairly easy gather, considering that the country was mostly rolling hills with a few cedar and piñon trees scattered about. But it did require a lot of riding to cover the country adequately. And the cattle knew where they were going. Colder nights and cooler days signaled that the fall was already here and winter would soon be coming.

I met up with David and we visited for a few minutes. David told me, "We've about covered all the country. You make one more circle around to where you meet the fence. The fence runs east and west. Bring the cattle you find along the fence to the east. Eventually, you'll meet me again and we'll follow the fence until we meet Sheila in the corner. After we put the cows through the gate, we'll about be done for the day."

I did as I was told, found a few more cattle, and soon met up with David. We moved our cattle toward the corner where we saw Sheila, loosely holding all the cattle in the corner.

Along the way, David asked, "How's your horse holding up?"

"He's a little tired," I replied. "But this has done him some good. He's starting to respond to leg pressure and he's watching the cattle. With more riding, he'll be a good horse."

We reached the corner where Sheila was holding the cattle.

"I'll ride through, open the gate and count them through," said David. "Don't let them come too fast."

David counted the cattle at the gate. When the last cow had passed through, he rode over to where Sheila and I were waiting. He had a big smile on his face.

"This has been the most successful gather I've ever had. If my count's right, we're only short about fifty head. Will, are you sure you got all the cattle off the west side?"

"I can't guarantee that," I said. "I only started a few bunches to the east. There could be a lot of cattle over there yet."

"We'll have to ride that tomorrow," he said. "We'll go back to the ranch, get another truck and go to the windmill tonight and get the two-ton. We'll truck our horses tomorrow back to the windmill and ride the west side."

I'd been watching the sky. Dark clouds were forming and to me, it looked like we were about to get some snow.

"How long before the snow flies?" I asked.

David glanced up at the sky. "Probably tomorrow," he said. "Better dress warm. It's liable to get cold tomorrow."

After we got back to the ranch, grained our horses and turned them loose, I volunteered to ride back to the windmill with David to bring back the two-ton truck. It would mean an extra-long day, but I thought if he could do it, so could I.

I drove the two-ton truck back to the ranch. It was well after dark when we got back and after supper I went straight to bed.

The next day I saddled Bay for the day's gather. There was a small skiff of snow on the ground and I thought there would be more at the windmill. It wasn't snowing, but the threat of more snow lingered in the clouds overhead.

All summer long I'd been using my chink chaps, but this morning, I went to the car and got out my shotgun chaps, which would be warmer.

David, Sheila, and I loaded our horses in the two-ton and started out for the windmill, taking the road through the BLM ground. It was rough going. The road was slick with a little snow on it, but David took it easy.

"As late as we are getting here," said David, "I think it best that we just start what cattle we find to the east, and meet here and take the truck back to the ranch. We'll push the cattle as far to the east as we can and hopefully they'll continue to drift to the east and south. We'll come back tomorrow and gather them up."

There were some cows and calves watering at the windmill. "Sheila," said David, "you start these cattle east. Will and I will ride around and see what we can gather up."

David and I started toward the west, figuring on making two big circles and meeting up with Sheila later in the day. As we left, David said, "I wish I'd have left the tent and cooking equipment up here. We could have camped here and rode this country more thoroughly."

We rode for a while in silence. It was cold and snowing lightly. There wasn't much sense in discussing the weather, there wasn't much either one of us could do about it. The cold weather convinced me that I should be heading south toward a warmer climate for the winter.

We split up, David going north and I went south. I found a few cattle and pushed them east. I thought it best if I stayed fairly close to the cattle for fear of losing them. I hate to go out to gather cattle and not show up with anything.

I soon found Sheila with the cattle she'd started from the windmill and put the cattle I'd found with hers.

"Have you seen David?" she asked.

"Not since we split up," I answered. "I'll ride off to the north an' see if I can find him. It's gettin' late enough, we ought to start headin' home."

"I'll keep going east," said Sheila. "I think it's getting colder."

"Yes, ma'am."

I rode off to the north, looking for more cattle and David. I mused to myself, *Sheila shouldn't be worried about David bein' lost. He knows this country. Course, his horse could have fallen an' he could be hurt somewhere.*

I finally found David. He was pushing a larger bunch of cattle than Sheila and I had both found and having a hard time. The cattle didn't want to move.

I helped him. When we got to where we could talk, I said, "If we push these cows a little more to the southeast, we'll meet up with Sheila. She's only a mile an' a half off in that direction."

"That's what I've been trying to do, but the cattle aren't co-operating," he said. "With your help, it should be easier."

We moved the cattle toward where I expected to meet Sheila. She'd made better progress than I figured and was about two miles away. We mixed our cattle with hers and David said, "I think we'll just leave these cattle here, they should drift toward the corner fence. We'll come up tomorrow and push them the rest of the way."

We rode back to the windmill, loaded our horses in the truck and headed toward the home ranch. We'd put in another long day.

The next day at breakfast, David informed me that he'd convinced Sheila that he and I could handle the day's gather alone. It was cold and there was about six inches of snow on the ground. I thought that he was just trying to make things easy for his wife, which was nice.

We rode horseback to where we'd left the cattle the day before. They'd continued to drift toward the corner fence. We went farther back to the west, just to make sure we hadn't lost any cattle.

We pushed the cattle toward the corner in the fence and David counted them through the gate. "According to my count, we're still missing some cows," he said. "Tomorrow, we'll gather the holding pasture, move them across the road, corral them and sort off the calves. I'll have the farm hands put out enough hay to handle the calves overnight and call the cattle buyers. We should be able to ship the calves over the next few days."

"What about the cattle that are still missin'?" I asked.

"They've either died, strayed onto the BLM ground, or the neighbors have gathered them. If they're still on our range, they'll wander home as it gets colder or more snow falls. We're about done."

I welcomed the news. I wasn't too keen on spending more time in the cold country. I was ready for warmer climates.

The next day, Sheila, David, and I saddled our horses and gathered the holding pasture. In comparison to the way things had been going, it was a fairly easy morning. We had the cattle corralled before noon. We hobbled our horses and turned them loose in a separate pen. As we ate our noon meal, which Sheila had fixed, David explained the chores for the afternoon.

"Will," he said, "you'll work the gate for the calves. Sheila can work the gate for the bulls and whatever else. We'll have a few of the neighbor's cows that Sheila can take. I'll bring the cattle to you horseback and holler which way they're supposed to go. We should be able to sort everything before dark."

I took off my chaps and hung them on the fence. Working a gate while sorting the cattle was a lot of groundwork, and the shotgun chaps would be a hindrance.

We started sorting cattle. With the fresh snow on the ground and the ground fairly warm, it wasn't long before my lower legs were covered in mud. My boots were soaked clear through. It was a miserable afternoon.

At one point, David volunteered to swap positions with me but I declined saying, "I'm already covered in mud. No sense in you gettin' the same way."

It took us the rest of the afternoon, but we sorted all the calves from the cows. We then sorted the bulls from the neighbor's cows and a few cull cows.

"I'll call the cattle buyers tonight," said David, "and tell them they can come and get the calves. And I'll call the neighbors and tell them we've got some of their cattle. When everything is loaded, we'll be done."

We turned the cattle out and opened the gates to the hayfields. The cattle would find their own way to them. They'd winter on them.

The following morning, David told me, "The semis that the calf buyer uses aren't going to be here until day after tomorrow. We'll take tomorrow off then load calves the next day."

"What day of the week is it?" I asked. I tended to lose track of time when I was out on the ranch. I hadn't known what day of the week it was all summer while I was in camp.

"It's Thursday," replied David. "We should be done by Sunday."

I spent the next day relaxing and doing a little laundry. All I had to do before I left was put my saddle and bedroll in the car and go. I was getting anxious to leave.

On Saturday the semis arrived. The place looked like a used truck and trailer lot. We went right to work loading the trailers. As soon as one trailer was loaded and pulled away, another one was ready to back up to the chute and be loaded. The drivers would yell out how many calves they wanted for each section of the trailer. Sheila would push them out into the alleyway, David would count them, and I pushed them toward the trailer. The drivers would load them, then close the partitions inside the trailer. These cattle were calves, although most of them were as big as their mothers.

I did a lot of walking that day, as did everyone else. We didn't bring horses. I noticed that David and Sheila were almost as muddy as I was the afternoon we sorted the calves. I laughed a little, until I looked at myself. I had about as much mud on me as they did.

We loaded cattle all day, and by nightfall, we'd loaded all the calves. We drove home in the pickup and on the way David said, "I suppose you'll be leaving in the morning."

"Yep," I replied.

"You know," continued David, "you've got a job here all winter if you want it."

"Yep," I answered. "But I think I'd rather spend the winter somewhere where it's warmer."

"I'll have your paycheck ready in the morning, after breakfast. You might as well relax tomorrow, then leave Monday, if you must. You can't cash the check until Monday anyway."

"I'll probably just do that," I said.

The next morning, after breakfast, David handed me my check. "There's a little bonus in it. It isn't much, but it's all I can spare until I get a check for the calves."

David spent the rest of the morning trying to convince me to stay the winter, but I was firm in my decision to leave. When he saw that I wasn't going to change my mind, he said, "If you show up around the first of March next year, you'll have a job. We'll be calving then and we've got branding, and they'll always be salt to pack and cattle to move."

"How do you do your brandin'?" I asked.

"We have a calf table," answered David.

A red roper, I thought to myself. *There ain't any ropin' an' draggin' calves to a fire. I can almost guarantee that I won't be here.*

"Well," I told David, "next year is a long way off. It's hard to say what will happen between now and then."

David gave me his mailing address and said, "Keep in touch."

I loaded my saddle, blankets, and other equipment in the trunk of the car that night. All I would have to load after breakfast was my bedroll and shaving equipment.

Dude Wrangler

I loaded my bedroll before breakfast the next day. At breakfast, David was still trying to convince me to stay. I was actually becoming a little perturbed at his persistence, although I really liked him. When we finished eating, I shook his hand and Sheila offered hers and I shook it. Without any further talk, I went to the car, started it and drove off.

I would go to town, cash my check, get a haircut, then drive farther south and look for work. I kinda regretted leaving the Browns, they were nice people. A lot nicer than most of the people I'd met or worked for the previous winter.

I drove south for a couple of days, stopping occasionally to see if anyone had a riding job available. I didn't have any luck, so I kept going south.

I finally ended up in what I was told was the dude ranch capitol of the world. At the employment agency, they told me that there weren't any riding jobs available with cattle, but they said I might get on with a dude ranch guiding the "guests" around. They told me that, "You don't refer to the dudes as dudes, but guests." I failed to see the difference. They gave me a list of the ranches that might be looking for dude wranglers and directions to each one.

I started driving, intending on hiring on with one of the dude ranches. I got hired last fall at one dude ranch, but when I showed up to start work, I was told that the place had been sold and they didn't have a position for me. That was the beginning to my spending some time in jail, through no fault of my own.

The first dude outfit I drove into was immaculate looking. Lawns were kept mowed and trimmed. Someone had put in a lot of time developing the landscape around the main lodge, and a lot of time maintaining it. It looked like a high-class place to me.

I found the foreman, introduced myself and asked if he were doing any hiring.

The foreman, his name was Jacobson, invited me in for a cup of coffee, and then said, "Tell me about yourself. You look like a cowboy, but this job requires some people skills most cowboys don't have."

I told him about my previous experience. It was all with cattle or horses on ranches. I'd never worked on a dude outfit.

"Guest ranch," he corrected.

"Yes sir," I said. I'd been warned before, but it slipped my mind.

I purposely omitted my stint in jail. I was told it wouldn't show up on my record. But Mister Jacobson caught me by surprise.

He asked, "Have you ever been convicted of a crime?"

I hesitated for a moment, then said, "Yes."

I explained my predicament with Butch Wolfe and the resulting consequences of it.

"So you worked for Butch Wolfe, huh?" questioned Mister Jacobson.

"Yes sir," I replied. "Do you know him?" I started thinking that if Mister Jacobson knew Butch Wolfe, I didn't want to work for him.

"I've only met him once or twice. He tried to sell me some horses and if remember right, he couldn't get a brand inspection or whatever. They looked to be pretty good horses. Anyway, I didn't buy anything from him. I know him mostly by reputation, and that isn't very good. Wasn't there something in the paper about him and his bunch being arrested about a year or so ago?"

"I don't know," I said, "I was in jail. I didn't see any newspapers. But the judge and my lawyer told me about it. Mister Wolfe is expected to be in jail himself for a very long time."

Mister Jacobson laughed. "I'd like to hire you, but can't. If my employers, the owners, found out I'd hired a jailbird I'd be in trouble. And they'd find out, eventually. They have a background check done on every prospective hire. While I personally think you're all right, I know the owners would frown on your hire. You might try down the road. There's another dude ranch ..."

"Guest ranch," I interrupted.

Mister Jacobson laughed. "Yes, guest ranch. They're about twenty miles down the road. I don't know what their hiring policies are. I'll give them a call and let them know you're coming. Let me know how you make out."

I thanked Mister Jacobson for his time and started for the next ranch, a little discouraged. If everyone did a background check, I might have a hard time getting a job.

The next ranch wasn't as well kept as the first place I went to. As I drove in, I saw a group of riders leaving. I stopped and watched as they passed. I sized up all the riders and thought I knew why they were called dudes. As I sized up the dudes, I also looked over the horses. They were all in good shape and seemed well mannered.

I found the owner and introduced myself. His name was Bill Davis.

"I've been expecting you," he said. "Craig called and said you'd be showing up."

"Craig?" I questioned.

"Craig Jacobson, the foreman up the road. I'd have gone with those folks you saw leaving as you were coming in, but Craig said it might be worth my time to talk to you. Tell me about yourself."

Apparently, in spite of my jailbird record, I'd made a favorable impression on Mister Jacobson. I outlined my experience much the same as I did for Craig Jacobson. I didn't skip over the part about working for Butch Wolfe.

"So you worked for Butch Wolfe. That ain't much of a

recommendation. You know, that no good lying, dirty ... well we're not really supposed to use language like I was going to use on the dude ranch. But he ain't no good! You know that dirty so and so, he tried to sell me a horse he'd stolen from me. When he found out I already owned the horse, he changed his story. He tried to make me believe he found the horse out on the highway. What did you do for him?"

"I drove a truck for him for three days, only I didn't know the truck was stolen an' the horses I was haulin' were stolen. I was arrested for that and spent some time in jail for it. But I'm out now."

"What's Butch doing?"

"Time," I said. "He's still in prison."

"How'd you get out, escape?"

I laughed, then explained how the judge offered me a job, taking care of the horses I was supposed to have stolen.

Bill laughed. "That sounds like Maggie."

"Maggie? Who's that?" I asked

"Maggie McAdams, she was probably your judge."

"McAdams was the name of my judge, but I wasn't on a first name basis with her," I said.

Bill laughed again. "I have been looking for another hand," he said. "I suppose I could hire you on a trial basis. If you fit in with the hands and dudes, you've got a job, but just for the winter. If not, you'll be free to go, no hard feelings."

"That's fair enough," I said. "Mister Jacobson wanted me to let him know how I made out here. Could you call him for me?"

"No need to," said Bill. "I told him I'd hire you if I liked you. He told me I would. Put your stuff in the bunkhouse. You got your own saddle?"

"Yes sir," I said.

"Put it in the barn. I'll show you around if you want. We'll be eating in about an hour and a half."

I put my bedroll in the bunkhouse and my saddle in the

barn and as Bill showed me around, he explained a little about the operation.

"We saddle the horses we need before breakfast every morning. Everything is kept in the corral. We feed the horses morning and night. We'll feed the saddled horses. After breakfast, the folks that want to ride will come down to the corrals at the times they've indicated. Our rides are scheduled. One-hour rides leave at nine, eleven, one-thirty and three-thirty. Two-hour rides leave at ten and two. Longer rides can be scheduled as time and help permit. You'll get a chance to accompany each ride to learn the trails. Each ride goes to a different destination.

"Our horses are pretty gentle," continued Bill. "But occasionally we have to discipline or tune up a horse. We don't do that in front of the dudes. We don't need any showoffs in this business, they tend to cause wrecks. Safety is of the utmost importance. We're pretty laid back, but do follow a regular routine. Any questions?"

"What time do we start in the mornin'?"

"We'll start at five."

"I'll be ready," I said.

Supper was at six and the hired help ate separately from the dudes. I met the other wranglers. There was Nick, he was older and appeared to be the wrangler boss. There was Don, he appeared to be a regular guy. Charlie was a quiet, middle-aged man and he appeared to have had plenty of horse experience. The youngest of the wranglers was Rudy. He was barely out of his teens. If anyone was going to be a showoff or prankster, I figured it would be Rudy.

I ate supper, answering questions about myself from the other hands. Rudy was the most inquisitive. He had a lot of questions and many of them didn't pertain to the work I was going to do or what I'd done. I had an immediate dislike for him, but decided to conceal my feelings.

The next morning, Nick had a list of the horses we were

expected to use. Apparently he'd talked with Bill and got the list of people that were scheduled to ride. Of course I didn't know any of the horses, but Nick would catch one, halter him, tell me his name and I'd go saddle him. Each horse got the same saddle every day and the horse's name was on the saddle rack. A bridle was tied to each saddle on the left side. When we'd about saddled all the dude horses, Nick handed me a horse.

"This is Sleepy," he said. "You put your saddle on him."

Sleepy, I thought. *I wonder what they take me for.*

"Don't let the name fool you," said Nick, as he noticed the apprehensive look on my face. "He's all horse."

After what Nick told me, I expected some problems. I started to hobble the horse, but Charlie stopped me. "You don't need to hobble these horses. They're saddled almost every day."

I saddled the horse without any problem and turned him loose with the other saddled horses and we went to breakfast. I'd noticed that Rudy wasn't as fast as the other fellers saddling horses. Every time he finished saddling a horse, he'd step back and look at what he'd done, much like an artist stepping back to admire his work. I thought this was a little bit strange, but never said anything to anybody about it.

We saddled about thirty-five horses that morning, plus the horses we were going to ride.

"You're going to ride Sleepy today, huh?" asked Rudy.

"Yep," I answered. I wanted to ask him what the horse was like, but kept quiet. The immediate dislike I'd developed for him prevented me.

"I've always wanted to ride him," continued Rudy, "but Nick never gave him to me."

"Oh," I said, curiously. I wondered why.

At breakfast Bill told me, "We always have somebody holding the horse when the dudes are getting on, for safety purposes. And we never let anyone get on while the horse is tied to the rail. And always check the cinch before a person gets on."

This was obvious to me and I thought Bill was just trying to stress the safety aspect of this business.

"When the dudes are getting on," continued Bill, "hold the saddle in place. Dudes tend to pull themselves into the saddle, rather than spring up. Pulling the saddle toward themselves while they're getting on causes saddle sores over time."

We finished breakfast and went down to the corrals to wait for the dudes to show up for their rides.

Nick said to me, "You'll go on the first hour ride with Don. Pay attention and learn the trail. Just ride alongside and keep an eye on things. You might want to step on your horse in the round corral before the dudes show up. He's all right, but he hasn't been rode for a while."

Without asking any questions, I got Sleepy, took him in the round pen, tightened the cinch and untracked him. All the hands were lined up outside the round pen, watching. I noticed this and immediately became a little suspicious, expecting the worst.

While I was walking him around, Rudy said, "Go ahead, get on him!"

Charlie reprimanded Rudy, saying, "Be quiet, he knows what he's doing."

Satisfied that I'd moved the horse around enough, I stopped him and stepped on. I felt the horse tense up as I settled in the saddle. I sat there for minute, shifting my weight in the saddle. When I felt the horse relax a little, I moved him out at a walk. I walked him around the corral, turning him both ways and stopping him. He seemed to be well broke. I urged him into a trot and he hesitated a little, but moved out. Slowly, I felt him relax.

"He should be all right now," said Nick. "Just keep an eye on him."

Rudy appeared to be disappointed that the horse didn't do anything when I topped him off.

The dudes started arriving for the nine o'clock ride. Each

guest was assigned a horse that he or she would ride each time for the duration of their visit. Not knowing any of the guests or the horses, Nick had me help a lady on her horse, Dynamite.

"I just love him," she said as she approached the horse. "Isn't he beautiful?"

I looked the horse over and didn't see any outstanding features. But I agreed with the lady.

While I was helping the lady on, I noticed that Rudy had a dude mounted on his horse while the horse was still tied to the rail. I started to slip quietly over to where the horse was tied, but Nick got there first. He untied the slipknot on the halter, gave Rudy a dirty look and walked away, shaking his head disgustedly.

Don and I both mounted our horses. Don gave some real brief instructions and we started out. It was a slow, walking ride. I rode alongside, keeping an eye on the dudes and their equipment. I answered questions from the dudes but was reluctant to ask any questions other than "Where you from?" I wasn't good at making conversation.

About fifteen minutes away from the barn, Don stopped the ride.

"What's up?" I asked.

"Cinch check," answered Don as he got off his horse. "We always check cinches about ten or fifteen minutes out."

I went to the tail end of the ride, got off and started checking cinches. I didn't find anything wrong, but as I approached Don, I could hear him muttering something about "Rudy not doing his job!" as he was pulling a cinch a couple of holes tighter.

We continued on the ride. A little farther along the trail, Don motioned me forward. "This is where you'll go off on the two-hour ride. It circles around and rejoins this trail before we get back to the barn."

I nodded and went back to the tail end of the ride. Things were going smoothly.

Our ride ended back at the barn. It was uneventful.

Bill was at the barn and he said to me, "You'll go on the two-hour ride with Don at two o'clock. What did you think of that trail?"

"It was easy enough an' kinda scenic," I said.

"That's just what we want," said Bill. "Relaxing, enjoyable rides with no problems."

Don was listening. "Well, we do have a problem," he said.

"Oh?" said Bill. "What is it?"

"That Rudy. He's not tightening cinches. I saw Missus Murphy leaning in the saddle. If we hadn't stopped when we did, she'd have fallen off. And this morning, he put Mister Erickson on his horse while the horse was still tied to the rail. Will, here, started to slip over and untie the horse, but Nick got there first. That kid is an accident looking for a place to happen."

"I'll talk with Nick about it," said Bill. "How did Will get along?"

"Fine," answered Don. "He's a hand. He shouldn't have any problems."

We hung around the barn and helped the one-hour riders off their horses that had left at eleven with Charlie. The two-hour ride that had left at ten showed up and we helped them off their horses. We loosened cinches on all the horses and tied their bridles to the saddles. We ate our noon meal at twelve-thirty.

Rudy had been on the two-hour ride with Nick, and it was obvious as Rudy helped people off their horses that he was working for tips. I thought it kind of distasteful, but didn't say anything. To me, it appeared that Rudy was trying to be a cowboy and he knew he wasn't.

"Everything go all right?" Bill asked Nick when all the riders were off and we were making our way to the lodge for lunch.

I followed Bill and Nick and overheard their conversation.

"No," answered Nick. "That Rudy has only been here three days and he's caused more problems than I've seen in three years. He doesn't listen to instructions. He runs his horse around the dudes. He's a showoff and he's going to cause some real serious problems. I've told you about them every day."

"Well," said Bill, "now that Will's here, I think we can let him go."

"You never should have hired him in the first place!" said Nick. "He's no hand. Besides that, he's bad luck!"

"How's he bad luck?"

"At the end of the day, he throws his hat on the bed and his spurs on the floor. Every cowboy knows its bad luck to put your hat on a bed. I told him more than once it would be easier on him if he threw his hat on the floor and his spurs on the bed. It wouldn't be near as painful when he got out of bed in the morning," said Nick.

"Throwing his hat on the bed isn't a good reason to fire him. But the other reasons are. You know, when I hired him, I only hired him on the basis that if he worked out, he'd have a job. If he didn't, we'd let him go," said Bill. "And, we needed help at the time. We'll still need one more hand if you guys want a day off every week."

"Yeah," said Nick. "But as far as I'm concerned, you can't let him go fast enough!"

"I'll fire him right after dinner," said Bill.

Overhearing the conversation, I felt a little guilty, feeling that I was the cause of Rudy's getting fired. I talked to Bill about it.

"I overheard your talk with Nick about Rudy," I said. "I hope my showin' up ain't caused you extra problems."

"No," replied Bill. "I had my doubts about Rudy when I hired him and never should have done it. I thought when I hired you, we were set for the winter, but I've had too many complaints from the other hands about him. I would have had to let him go anyway. You just came and filled a hole that was about to be emptied. He'll be gone by one o'clock, right after dinner."

After we ate, Nick, Charlie, Don, and I went to the barn to get ready for the afternoon rides. Bill called Rudy into his office for a private conversation.

When Rudy came to the barn, with a look of bewilderment on his face, he said, "Bill fired me! I'll get my saddle and stuff and leave."

"I'll give you a hand," said Nick. Charlie, Don, and I followed, just to make sure Rudy only took his stuff. When he had his saddle in the car, we all followed him to the bunkhouse to help him, and keep an eye on his actions.

"I don't know where to go from here," said Rudy.

I sort of felt sorry for him, even though I didn't much care for him. "There are some ranches looking for cattle feeders up north," I said.

I debated about telling him about the place I'd left where the boss conducted his business from a pickup truck and the cook was a wino. Then, I thought, *Why not? He can't do a lot of damage up there.*

I gave Rudy directions to the place. He thanked me and left. I didn't know if I might be playing a cruel joke on the ranch owner or Rudy.

I went on the two-hour ride with Don. It was a more scenic ride than the one hour, but not any more difficult, just twice as long.

Because Rudy was gone, Bill took out a one-hour ride.

When we got back to the barn, Don said, "Tomorrow, you'll get a chance to see the other trails. We take different trails each day. You'll soon know all of them and probably find them boring. But the dudes like them."

The New Hand

Each day was the same routine. One day a dude asked me, "Have you lived here all your life?"

Without thinking, I said, "Not yet."

The dude thought that was hilarious and I worried that he might fall off his horse, he was laughing so hard.

"I guess I asked for that," he said when he stopped laughing. He rephrased his question, asking, "Where are you from?"

I told him and gave him a brief description of what I'd been doing. I left out the part about being in jail.

The dudes provided some interesting moments. One asked, "When is that gelding going to have a colt?"

I laughed at that one pretty hard myself, then stated, after I regained my composure, "Geldings don't have colts." The horse was overly fat.

I found it interesting that quite often the dudes tried to be something they weren't around the horses. There seemed to be something unique or special about being an accomplished horseman—probably a holdover from the old horse and buggy days.

According to Bill, we were still one man short of having a full crew, although I didn't notice any unduly heavy workloads. Each hand got about three hours of riding each day, and it was all walking, so they were easy rides.

I was surprised when Bill showed up one morning and announced that he'd hired another person. I was even more surprised when he said his new hand was a girl! He explained, "She's a college student and is sitting out the winter from school due to lack of funds."

I was about to ask, "Where's she goin' to stay?" There was no room in the bunkhouse for a woman.

I guess I had a look of curiosity on my face, because Bill said, "She'll stay up at the main lodge with the maids."

There were three girls working as maids at the ranch and they also doubled as food servers. Bill's wife supervised them.

"She'll be here tomorrow, about noon," said Bill. "You boys give her a hand and make her feel welcome. She comes highly recommended."

I was out on a ride the next day when she showed up. She had put her personal stuff up in the lodge and was saddling a horse when I arrived. I watched her throw her saddle on a horse and saw that she was experienced.

Bill was telling her, "You'll ride Dopy. We've named all the guide horses after the seven dwarfs or flowers. Will here is riding Sleepy. Nick rides Petunia, although he calls him Pete. We've named all the dude horses with more threatening sounding names, like Hurricane, or Tornado, or Widow Maker. It's kinda humorous to see the reaction of the dudes when we tell them they're riding Suicide or Coffin or Cadaver. But don't let the names of the guide horses fool you, they're all good horses."

After introductions we went to the lodge to eat. We ate our noon meal and the new hand, her name was Julie, ate with us wranglers. It was a quiet meal. None of the men wanted to appear overly inquisitive. Finally, Bill broke the silence when he said, "Julie, tell us something about yourself."

"I'm a student at the state college, majoring in Animal Science. I plan on managing the family ranch when I graduate. I'm taking a year off because I've run a little short of money. I was planning on becoming a vet, but it appears that will be cost prohibitive."

"Won't taking a year off interrupt your studies?" asked Don.

"No. I've completed all my required classes, Math, English and the like. When I go back, I can concentrate on my major classes."

"What kind of ranch does your family have?" asked Nick.

"We have a cow-calf operation up north," replied Julie. "We've got about four hundred fifty, five hundred cows."

"What's your experience been?" asked Nick.

"Mostly just on our ranch. There's plenty to do there and my brothers have all decided on different careers. I'm the only one left."

Bill and Nick asked a lot of questions and Don, Charlie, and I just listened. It appeared that Julie had a lot of experience with horses and cattle.

Bill asked, "What kind of entertainer are you?"

"I do play a guitar, a little," she replied.

"You'll get a lot of experience with people in this job," said Bill. "In fact, it'll start right now. You'll go out with Charlie on the one-hour ride at one-thirty. Pay attention and learn the trail. We have a different trail for each of our rides."

We left the dinner table and went to the barn. Riders were starting to gather to go out on their rides.

As we got the riders on their horses, Bill explained the procedure to Julie. "Tighten the cinch, hold the saddle in place while the person is climbing on. Now get your horse and follow Charlie and the dudes. Learn the trail."

I watched as Julie put on her chaps. They were chinks and showed plenty of use. She got on her horse. From the way she got on, I could tell she'd had plenty of horse experience. The other hands were watching also, and Julie met their approval.

The ride left and those of us left behind got ready for the two o'clock ride. I was scheduled for the two-hour ride. There were only three people on it and I took it out alone.

I thought I'd learned all the different trails and some I liked better than others. Nick assigned the rides in a manner that no one rode the same trail repeatedly. And everyone got about three hours of riding every day, a one-hour ride and a two-hour ride. I thought I had the routine down fairly well when I was thrown a curve.

Bill came down to the barn one morning and announced, "We'll have a steak fry ride tonight. There won't be a two-hour ride at two. Everyone will need to go, especially if you want to eat. Julie, you bring your guitar."

"But I'm not really an entertainer," protested Julie.

"You said you played a little. Now you'll have a chance to entertain—a little!" said Bill.

"What's a steak fry ride?" I asked Nick after Bill made the announcement.

"Well," he said, "we take everybody out for about an hour ride and end up at a cookout area—there's picnic tables there. The cook will be there, he takes the groceries out in the pickup. He'll cook steak, beans, corn on the cob and we'll eat supper there. There's a hitch rail where we can tie the horses. We'll do it every Friday night for the rest of the season."

"Is today Friday?" I asked. "I tend to lose track of time on the ranch."

"Yep," replied Charlie. "You'll be reminded every Friday morning from now on. We leave at four, that's why there's no two o'clock two-hour ride. It'll take about an hour to get there, it takes about an hour to eat and about half an hour to get back. We might be a little longer depending on how much poetry Don recites."

"Half an hour to get back? How come?" I asked.

"We take a short cut," replied Charlie. "You haven't been on those trails yet."

I laughed. I didn't know as much as I thought I did. "Don's a poet?"

"Yep. He's pretty good, too! After you hear him a couple of times, you'll probably get tired of his poetry, but frequently, he comes up with something new."

"How come every Friday?" I asked.

"Generally, folks come on Sunday and leave Saturday. Having the cookout on Friday kinda gives everyone a good send-off.

111

Those folks that stay a couple of weeks or a month or so, they get to do it more than once."

At four o'clock, we had the dudes and the maids mounted on their horses and started out. The cook had loaded the supplies and Julie's guitar in the pickup and was already at the cookout area when we arrived. The fires were going, the steaks were cooking, and so were the corn and beans.

We got the maids off their horses first. They were going to serve the food. Then we got the dudes off and they made their way to the cooking area.

By the time the wranglers made it to the cookout area, the dudes had gotten their food and were eating. We went through the line. The cook put our steaks on the plates and the maids served up the corn and beans.

As she dished out beans, Susie, one of the maids, made the comment, "This is really neat! The guests come to us for their food, rather than us taking their food to them!" All the hands laughed at her comment.

After supper, Don recited some of his poetry. Julie sort of accompanied him on the guitar and it was quite pleasant.

Bill caught me by surprise when he asked, "Will, do you sing?"

"No sir," I replied. "I only know two songs, one of 'em is Yankee Doodle an' the other ain't!"

It was an old, old joke, but it brought a good laugh.

The winter wore on. The nights were cool, but there was little frost in the morning. The days were nice, warmer than it was up north, where it was twenty or thirty below zero in the mornings.

The dudes arrived on Sunday mornings and generally left on Saturday. It was a pretty pleasant winter.

Christmas came and went with all the decorations. Some of the guests spent every Christmas at the ranch. The hands decided that there would be no gift exchanges among themselves.

That was fine with me, I had all I needed and didn't want for more.

New Year's came and there was some partying at the lodge, but I didn't join in. There were fewer horse riders the first day of the New Year and I attributed that to some heavy drinking the night before.

The year started off uneventful, although Don did have a lady fall off her horse. Apparently the horse shied when a deer jumped up beside the trail and the woman fell off. She wasn't seriously injured, although she was a little sore for a few days.

A Nice Surprise

One day, Bill came up to me and said, "Will, we have one of your old friends coming in for a week. Make sure you show her every courtesy."

I was kind of surprised at the comment and the request. I wondered, *Why would he tell me this and why the request for extra courtesy? And who was she? I didn't have any lady friends in this part of the country.* Curiosity filled my mind and after every ride that I took out, I looked over the parking lot to see if I recognized any of the vehicles.

While I was helping riders off the eleven o'clock ride I had taken out, Bill approached with a strangely familiar lady by his side. I had seen the woman before, but couldn't remember where or when. She looked vaguely familiar.

As they approached, Bill said, "Will, you remember Judge McAdams, don't you?" She stuck out her hand and I shook it. Of course I remembered her, she was the judge that presided over my horse stealing case. She sent me to jail! I didn't recognize her without her judge's robes.

"How are you doing?" she asked.

"I'm fine. How are you?" I replied.

"I'm doing fine. Are you staying out of trouble?" she asked.

"Yes ma'am," I replied. "You haven't seen me in your court, have you?"

The judge laughed. "No. But have you been in any other courts?"

It was my turn to laugh. "No," I replied.

"You know," said Bill, "it was Maggie here that recommended you for this position and on her recommendation I hired you. After I had talked to Craig Jacobson, I called Maggie."

"Well, I certainly appreciate that," I said. "Judge, you'll have to fill me in on what's been happenin' in the Butch Wolfe situation. I'm curious. Course, we'll have to do it kinda privately. I wouldn't want all the guests to know that I'm a jailbird."

"Former jailbird," corrected the judge.

"Yes ma'am," I respectfully replied.

Bill said, "You two can visit later. Right now, it's time to eat. Will, after the noon meal, I want you to take Maggie out on a special ride. She's been a regular visitor here for years."

Later that afternoon, I took the judge out for a ride. On the ride, she said, "Nancy says to say hello."

"Nancy?" I questioned.

"Yes, Nancy. Your court appointed lawyer."

"Oh, yes. How is she doin'?"

"She's fine," replied the judge. "She's expecting in May."

"Expecting? Expecting what?"

"A baby, of course! Are you really that far out of touch with normal people?"

"I guess so, although I wonder how many of these dudes are really normal." I said. "Would you tell her I said congratulations an' hope everything is okay?"

"Certainly," replied the judge.

"Now," I said, "if you would fill me in on what happened to Butch Wolfe, I'd appreciate it. I haven't heard any news about it since I left your probation officer."

"As you know, Mister Wolfe went to prison for a term of five years and his accomplice, I think his name was Shorty, went with him," said the judge. "The person you helped apprehend also went to prison, but he finally opened up to a prison guard and informed him that Mister Wolfe's partner, a Mister Butler, was the head of the outfit. He was located in another state and was already under arrest in connection with some drug charges. We'll have him extradited at the competition of his drug trial.

"If he implicates Mister Wolfe in connection with the illegal drugs, we'll get to try him again."

"This is gettin' more complicated the more I hear about it," I said.

"The legal system does get complicated," said the judge. "But everyone ends up getting a fair deal."

"Bill said that you were a regular guest out here," I said. "How long have you been comin' out here?"

"Actually, I've been coming out here for twenty, twenty-five years. Darlene, Bill's wife, is my sister."

"Oh," I said. "This is a small world. Do you know David or Sheila Brown?"

"No," said the judge. "Who are they?"

"They're the folks I worked for last summer, up north," I replied. "The way things are goin', I thought you might be related to them or know them."

The judge laughed. "What did you do for them?"

"Mostly packed salt an' fixed fence," I answered. "They're real nice folks. We actually caught some wild horses on his grounds."

"How did you do that?" asked the judge.

I explained how we built a trap around the waterhole, kept the horses off for a day or two, and then trapped them when they were thirsty.

"What did you do with them?"

"David called the BLM an' they came an' got 'em. I don't know what they did with 'em."

I rode with the judge for about two hours. She'd ridden quite a bit before. We had a good visit and I came to respect her a great deal. I never did hold any animosity toward her for sending me to jail. After all, she did arrange for me to take care of the horses I had supposedly stolen and I got paid for it!

The judge rode every day that she stayed at the ranch and I got to ride with her quite often. When she left, she handed me her business card and said, "When you land somewhere this summer, drop me a note so I can keep you informed of the horse stealing happenings in our county. Of course, you can always stop in and say hello. You will be welcome. However, you might not be as welcome if you show up as a suspect in a criminal case."

"Yes, ma'am," I said, laughing.

The judge left the ranch, inviting me to come back next winter.

The winter passed, mostly uneventful. Occasionally a guest would fall off a horse. For the most part they were unhurt. On one of Julie's rides, a youngster, a girl about seven, fell off her horse. Julie reported the incident to Bill.

The girl's mother had stayed at the lodge and when it was reported to her that her daughter had fallen off, she rushed down to the corral to check on her. She was quite concerned and kept asking, "Where did you land? Where did you land?"

The youngster answered simply, "On the ground."

Bill and Nick laughed at the girl's answer.

The mother, being very distraught, rebuked them both. "This is not funny!" stated the mother. "This is very serious!"

"You're right," said Bill. "But the girl wasn't hurt. She got back on her horse and rode him in. She's okay. She even wants to ride again this afternoon."

"We'll have to consider that this afternoon," replied the mother.

"It's important she ride again this afternoon. If you prevent her from riding, she may develop a fear of horses and may never ride again. It's important she ride this afternoon," replied Julie.

The mother relented, mostly at the insistence of her husband, and the young lady rode on the afternoon ride.

I was listening to the exchange between Bill and the girl's mother. When it was over, I asked, "How come that girl ain't in school?"

"She's being home schooled," answered Bill.

"Home schooled? What's that?" I asked.

"Parents that don't send their youngsters to a public or private school, they educate them at home."

"I never heard of that," I said.

"It's kinda new," said Bill.

"If they'd have had that when I went to school, all I'd have learned was how to load hay an' feed cows," I said. "I doubt I'd have gotten a degree in that!"

On the Wagon

As the winter passed, the days got longer. The nights were still quite cool, but the days were warm. There were only two mornings when there was frost on the windows of the cars in the parking lot all winter long.

We continued the steak fry rides. Earlier in the year, when we returned from the steak fries, it would be dark. Now, there was plenty of daylight left when we returned. The winter was winding down.

One night in March, Bill came to the bunkhouse. "The season's about over," he said. "Have you made plans for what you're going to do this summer?" he asked Don, Charlie, Julie, and myself. "We'll pretty much be done about the first part of April."

It was clear that Bill was giving us our walking papers. He was doing it in a nice way, preparing us.

"What are your plans, Don?" asked Bill.

"I've still got my summer job up on the rim," replied Don.

"And what about you, Charlie?"

"I'll go back to riding for the cattlemen's association on the forest service land," answered Charlie.

"And you, Julie?"

"I'll get a job in town and I plan on attending the summer semester at the university on a part-time basis. I can pick up a few classes then," she replied.

"And you, Will?"

"I ain't got no plans," I answered. "I'll head north until I find somethin'."

"You all know that I'd hire you all back next season," said Bill. "You've all got jobs."

"You know I'll be back," said Don.

"Me too," added Charlie. "I do it every year."

"I'll be in school all winter," said Julie.

"What about you, Will?" asked Bill.

"I don't make plans that far down the road," I said.

"You know you've got a job here next winter," said Bill.

"I appreciate that," I said. "I'll keep it in mind."

I started trying to plan for the spring and coming summer. In the middle of April, I doubted if anyone would be looking for help with their calving. But I might get hired on somewhere to help with branding.

I looked forward to heeling calves and dragging them to a branding fire. I hadn't even taken my rope off my saddle all winter and knew my roping would be very rusty, to say the least. As poor as I expected my roping to be, it would still be a lot of fun.

About the twelfth of April, the last of the dudes left the ranch. The place was strangely deserted and seemed like a ghost town compared to what had previously been a hub of activity.

At breakfast the next morning, Bill said, "The cook will be leaving in two more days and you all need to be gone by then. Take a day to relax then figure on being gone. I have your paychecks ready and have included a bonus for each one of you."

I thought it over and decided to leave that morning. I didn't need a day to relax or rest. The sooner I got on the road, the sooner I could find a summer job.

"I'll pick up my check after we're done here an' pull out this mornin'," I said.

I loaded my saddle, bedroll, and personal effects after breakfast, picked up my check and drove off. I noticed that Nick, Charlie, and Don came down to the barn when I loaded my saddle. I didn't take offense, I was the first to leave.

I headed north. The farther north I went, the more snow I noticed on the mountaintops. I didn't relish camping out, the nights were still quite cold, and so I got a motel room the first few nights.

I noticed small, white-faced calves in a lot of the fields as I drove. I figured the calving season was about over. Some of the calves had fresh brands on them and I knew I'd missed out on the branding.

I started stopping at employment agencies in some of the towns. I was looking for another riding job. I probably could have hired on a sheep outfit herding sheep, but I wasn't interested in that.

As I drove, I remembered that I'd intended to stop in the town where I'd been in jail and visit Judge McAdams, but I'd completely forgot about it. I still had her address and made up my mind to send her a letter when I found a job. I'd need to buy some paper and envelopes and did so in the next town I went through.

I finally found a job on a big cattle outfit in northern Nevada. I hired on as a buckaroo. I was told we were going to go out on the wagon, brand calves out in the open, pack a little salt, and move some cows around. It was a fairly large outfit—there were eight of us buckaroos, counting the cow boss. Some of the hands had worked the wagon on this ranch before and knew the country. Counting the cook, there would be nine of us out on the wagon.

I was told we would go out on the wagon in about a week. During that time, we branded a few calves that had wintered on the hay fields close to the home ranch. Everyone had a chance to rope calves and the other buckaroos had a chance to see just how rusty my roping really was.

Each morning, the cow boss would rope out our saddle horses from the remuda. We'd hobble the horses we saddled. After we untracked them, we'd get on then head out at a trot to do whatever we had to do that day. Quite often, we were done by two o'clock or two-thirty in the afternoon. On the way back to the ranch, about a hundred yards from the barn, it became a horse race. It wasn't really a horse race, but the buckaroos would run their horses toward the barn, then stop them and look at the horse tracks. It was a contest to see whose horse left the longest sliding stop tracks. The buckaroos were using the barn to help their horses stop. On one occasion, one guy couldn't get his horse to stop and the horse ran right through the open barn doors. We had a good laugh when the buckaroo came out, looking very embarrassed.

If any of our horses needed shoes, we'd put shoes on them in the afternoon. I didn't like shoeing horses when everyone else was shoeing. If another buckaroo got mad at the horse he was shoeing, he'd slap him with a rasp, and the horse would pull back and set off all the other horses. This caused quite a bit of confusion and all the horses became jumpy. It became more difficult to shoe the horses, even the gentler ones. I thought I'd have an easier time shoeing my string when there wasn't anyone else present, so that's what I did.

One afternoon, after a day's work, the cow boss said, "We're ready to go out on the wagon. All we need is a horse wrangler and I hired one earlier today. He'll be here day after tomorrow and we'll head out the next day. Have your stuff ready to load in the pickup."

The addition of the horse wrangler would make ten of us total.

I got the mailing address of the outfit and scribbled a short note to Judge McAdams, including the mailing address. I didn't have much to say other than I'd gotten a riding job. As an afterthought, I wrote,

> I haven't been in jail yet, but am not expecting to. I would have stopped in to see you, but didn't for two reasons. One, I was in a hurry to get up here and two, I thought that perhaps the offer of room and board in your facility might delay me longer. I prefer a motel where there ain't bars on the windows.

I signed the letter and had someone at the ranch mail it when he went to town.

The day after the horse wrangler arrived, we loaded our bedrolls in the pickup along with a big tent and the groceries that the cook would need. The cow boss led the remuda and the buckaroos followed, herding them. The cook followed the remuda in the truck. I noticed a lot of unbranded calves in the small bunches of cattle we passed along the way.

Around two in the afternoon, we arrived at what would be our first camp. I figured we were about eighteen or twenty miles from the home ranch. There was an old shack there and a handy corral and a fenced pasture. The cook put his bedroll in the shack along with the groceries. The horses would be turned out in the pasture at night and corralled in the morning. After we saddled our horses each morning, the rest of the remuda would be turned out to graze during the day and the horse wrangler would day-herd them.

On the first morning, I heard the cow boss tell the horse wrangler, "Don't let any of these horses go back to the home ranch! Keep them all fairly close, but let them graze. Bring them into the holding pasture about four o'clock."

The horse wrangler was on his horse and the cow boss opened the gate. The horses filed out slowly. They'd pretty much been there before. The rest of us buckaroos got on our horses. We were ready to go.

I had a pair of saddlebags on my saddle and was selected to carry the blackleg vaccine. The cow boss came over to me with the vaccine and said, "Put these in your saddlebags."

I was already mounted and said, "Go ahead, put 'em in. I ain't got anything in there other than a pair of gloves."

The cow boss was aware that a man didn't mess with another man's equipment and did as I told him.

We started out at a trot. We headed toward the home ranch to gather the cattle and unbranded calves that we'd passed yesterday. We got to where I'd first noticed the cattle and stopped. The cow boss started scattering riders, telling each one where to go and where we'd meet up.

We split up, each man going in the direction he was instructed. I was next to last to be told where to go. Everyone was told what direction to push the cattle and eventually we'd meet and hold a branding.

Little bunches of cattle started to merge as we progressed toward where we were to meet. Soon we were all gathered together and there were about a hundred head of cows. There were a lot of unbranded calves and a number of calves that had already been branded. We'd branded them in the corrals around the hay pastures and turned them out.

We didn't have a corral where we were to brand this bunch of calves. The cow boss selected one man to help him on the ground while branding, castrating, ear marking and vaccinating. He then picked two men to rope the calves. The rest of us spread out around the herd and kept them bunched.

Day herding these bunches of cattle was boring, but it was interesting watching the others rope. I decided that Steve, a Shoshoni Indian, was the best roper in the crowd. He rarely missed what he was throwing his loop at. However, he wasn't much good at day herding. I saw him sleeping in the saddle more than once and had to gather some cattle that thought they were escaping around him. I didn't say anything, which was the cow boss's job.

Everyone got a chance to rope and gradually my roping improved. I'd rope a calf, preferably by both his hind legs, dally up and drag him to the fire. The man helping the cow boss would hold the calf's head down while the cow boss vaccinated, branded, and castrated. He'd ear mark the calf by cutting off part of the ear leaving a specific pattern on what was left of the ear. He'd toss the pieces of ear he'd cut off in a pile and when we were through, he'd count the ears so we knew how many calves we'd branded. He'd enter this number in his tally book so he'd how many calves he had to ship in the fall.

We did this for three weeks steady, every day. We'd generally get done around two or three o'clock in the afternoon. We'd have to ride farther and farther from camp to find cattle each day, and soon we had to move camp.

Before we moved camp, a truck came from the home ranch with supplies for the cook, smokes for those buckaroos that smoked, and mail. I was surprised to get a letter.

I had to think a minute. Who knew I was here? Then I remembered that I'd sent a letter to Judge McAdams. Curious, I opened it and was relieved to find it wasn't a summons to appear in court.

The judge didn't have much to say, other than Nancy had a new baby girl. There were the customary questions like, "How are you doing?" and "When do you expect to be through here again?" She also wrote that there were no new developments in the Butch Wolfe case.

I thought it was kind of the judge to write me. I was surprised when the cow boss asked, "Anything serious?"

"No," I replied.

"I was curious," said the cow boss. "I noticed the return address on the envelope was a county court. Do you want to take a minute and write a reply? You in trouble?"

"No, on both counts," I replied. "Everything's all right."

We were going to move camp the next day, but it was raining. Rather than sit around in the big tent all day, the cow boss decided to gather the bulls and spread them out on the range.

Gathering the bulls was a job. The bulls were in good shape and some of them didn't want to go. It was dangerous. If a bull got whipped in a fight, he'd be mad and take off running. A feller didn't want to be in his way. He'd take out his revenge on anyone or anything handy. Everyone was warned more than once to give them plenty of room.

Frank didn't give a couple of bulls enough room and the loser in the bullfight took after him and his horse. They both managed to get away, but not before Frank's horse kicked the bull in the face. The bull almost got his head under the horse and the kick in the face was the horse's retaliation.

Everything turned out all right and Frank was careful to give all the bulls plenty of room. The cow boss reprimanded Frank severely and ended by saying, "No one was close enough to have helped you if that bull had upended you and the horse!"

Frank was embarrassed and said, "I guess you're right. I'll have to be more careful."

We moved the bulls quite a distance, but every now and then, we'd let some escape. They'd find the cows on their own. They didn't need much encouragement.

Occasionally, while we were out on the wagon, we'd see some wild horses. We'd run them, but never succeeded in getting close enough to rope one. It was fun, but the fact that we never caught one discouraged some of the hands.

"Don't be discouraged boys," Steve would say. "Them broom-tails have been run so much, they know all the tricks and the country to boot!"

The day after we moved bulls, it was not raining and we moved camp. I figured it was about another twenty miles from the home ranch. We had another corral and a holding pasture for the horses. There wasn't a cook shack, but we had another big tent for the cook to cook in. He also put his bedroll in the tent. His name was John.

The cook had a wood-burning stove to cook on. As primitive as the cooking facilities were, the groceries weren't. John was a baker by trade, but he also knew how to cook steak. John never cooked a bad meal for the buckaroos and he kept his baking skills in tune. Never before or since have I had homemade donuts, pies, sweet rolls, or cakes in a cow camp. All of the buckaroos appreciated it and quite often, when we were returning from a branding, we'd drag small trees or limbs that John could use for firewood. The cooking was the main reason all the buckaroos got along so well. Compared to some places I'd worked in the past, being out on the wagon on this outfit was a pleasure!

We'd been out on the wagon since April. I'd lost track of time. One night at supper, the cow boss said, "It's getting close to the first of June. We should be done by the fourth of July. Best be thinking about what you want to do the rest of the summer. We've got to gather and ship some yearlings when we get back to the ranch then we'll pretty much be done until the fall gather."

I hadn't given much thought to what I'd do when this job was over. I was enjoying the job and John's cooking too much.

The spring progressed and the routine stayed pretty much the same. On those days we couldn't brand because of rain, we packed some salt and scattered bulls. Nothing really exciting happened other than Steve's horse reared up and came over backward. Steve cleared the saddle, but landed on the barbed wire fence that was part of our night pasture. He wasn't hurt. He had a heavy coat on and the coat absorbed the barbs on the wire. He didn't even get a scratch.

On another occasion, Frank's horse started bucking one morning and bucked him off. He hit the ground pretty hard and let out a sorrowful moan when he landed. I wasn't too far away and my first impression was that he'd broken his hip. But he managed to get up and back on his horse.

I was thinking that a broken bone out here would be pretty serious. We had the pickup and could take the injured buckaroo to the ranch, but it would be a painful ride and might incur more damages.

We were branding calves one day and it was my turn to rope. The cow boss had just turned a calf loose that I'd dragged to the fire. I was coiling my rope and spotted an unbranded calf trotting alongside the herd. Without thinking, I made a half a loop and threw it at the calf. Much to my surprise, I caught the calf! With both hind legs! I dallied up and dragged the calf to the fire.

The cow boss and Pat were watching and when they saw I'd caught the calf, Pat asked, "What kind of throw do you call that?"

"I don't know," I replied. "It's a new one I been workin' on an' I ain't named it yet."

Thus the spring went. We branded a lot of calves and had a lot of fun. But it was drawing to a close. I didn't keep track, but I figured we'd branded about forty-five to sixty calves a day. It was a pretty big outfit.

The time finally came when we had to break camp and head to the home ranch. We trailed the horses back to the ranch, taking a different way than the way we'd come. The cow boss had the cook follow the horses in the truck.

We got to the ranch, turned the horses loose on good pasture and everybody went to the bunkhouse. The showers were pretty busy that night. The baths we'd had occasionally in the river were adequate, but cold and most of the fellers enjoyed a long hot shower. I thought that this ranch had a super duty hot water heater; nobody ran out of hot water even though some of the showers were kinda long.

The next day, the remuda was run in and we set out to gather the yearlings. Yearlings are a little harder to handle than cows, they need to be moved more slowly. If they were to start running for any reason, a feller would have his hands full holding them.

It took most of the day to gather the yearlings and I thought we had about eight or nine hundred head when we had them all. We had them all milling around in front of the gate to the big corral and as they circled around, they got closer to the gate. It would take some time, but eventually we'd have them corralled.

However, one of the hands got impatient. He took down his rain slicker, and waving it above his head, he let out a holler and rushed the cattle. Everybody yelled at him, "Stop!" but he didn't listen. He made a rush at the herd, trying to get the cattle to enter the corral, but didn't succeed in getting one yearling in.

As soon as he rushed the herd, the yearlings spooked and took off, running in all directions. The rest of us buckaroos couldn't hold them. They scattered, running as fast as they could go. It was as close to a stampede as I've ever seen, before or since.

The cow boss was disgusted. The hand who had lost his patience and rushed the herd was fired right on the spot.

"Get your saddle off that horse!" yelled the cow boss. "You're done!"

"But I'd have to walk back," complained the much embarrassed hand.

"That's right!" The cow boss yelled. "You've cost us an extra day. We'll have to regather these cattle tomorrow and the truckers will have to stay over! You've cost us too much!"

The hand got off his horse and unsaddled him.

"Your check will be at the office when you get there! Pick it up, leave and never come back!" The cow boss was still yelling and I don't remember ever seeing anybody as mad.

The next morning we saddled fresh horses and set out to gather the yearlings again. The semi-trucks that were to haul the yearlings had been parked by the corrals all night. The cow boss rode ahead and told them to move away from the corrals, shut the engines off, and stay in the trucks. After the problems we'd had yesterday, anything we could do to make corralling the cattle easier would be welcome.

We pushed the cattle toward the corrals and had them milling around the gate again. The more they milled around, the closer they got to the gate. Soon, a few more curious yearlings were looking into the corrals, investigating.

"Easy boys. They'll be going in soon," said the cow boss.

After another fifteen minutes or so, some of the yearlings entered the corral. The rest followed.

"Don't crowd them fellers, they'll all go given enough time," said the cow boss.

After what happened yesterday, nobody was in a rush today. When the last of the yearlings entered the corral and the gates were closed, the horses were hobbled, chaps came off and we made ready to load the cattle. The trucks were put in position. The cow boss stayed horseback and pushed cattle to the loading chute. I worked a gate, closing it behind the cattle the cow boss pushed toward the trucks. The driver of each truck told the cow boss how many cattle he wanted for each section of the trailer.

It took the rest of the day, but we loaded all the yearlings. As the trucks were loaded, they drove away toward the feedlot that would be the yearlings final home.

After the last yearling was loaded, we caught up our horses and rode back to the ranch. It was almost dark when we got there. After a late supper, everyone went to bed. It had been a long day and a lot of it on foot, which we weren't used to. We were tired.

I went to sleep, not knowing what to expect the next day.

At breakfast the next morning, the cook had fixed donuts and sweet rolls along with the regular ham and eggs. The cow boss went around and asked each hand, "Do you want to help with the hay?"

Most of the fellers answered "Yes." There were a few that declined.

I was asked, "Do you want to help with the hay?"

I replied, "No. I'll roll up."

After breakfast, those of us that decided to leave loaded our bedrolls and personal effects into our cars. We went to the barn, got our saddles, blankets, and bridles and loaded them into our cars under the watchful eyes of the cow boss and other hands that were staying on. I smiled to myself at the thought that even though we'd spent the last couple of months working together, nobody trusted anyone else enough to let them get their equipment unsupervised.

Looking for Work ... Again

I picked up my check at the office, shook hands with the rest of the crew, and drove off. My first stop would be at the first town I came to where I could cash my check. Then I didn't know what I'd do.

After I cashed my check, I went to the employment office to see about finding another job. There were a few jobs—working in the hay, fixing fence, and irrigating—but I wasn't interested in any of them. I drove off, still looking for work.

I had plenty of money, I didn't spend much, but I knew it wouldn't last forever. However, I wasn't concerned about finding a job.

I went to the Brown Ranch where I'd worked the summer before to see about working for them again and got hired on for the remainder of the summer, doing what I did the summer before. David Brown and his wife, Sheila, were happy to see me.

"You've got your old job back, if you want it," he said, hugging me enthusiastically.

I felt very uncomfortable being hugged by another man. It didn't seem to bother him.

Strange, I thought as his wife Sheila hugged me, *I feel almost as uncomfortable now with Sheila hugging me as I did when David hugged me.*

After the reunion was over, David said, "You can have your old horses back. I've been riding the black some and he's not bucking as much. The two bays haven't been ridden much. They might be a little tough to start with. The paint hasn't been used at all."

"I'll be lookin' forward to ridin' 'em," I said. "But I ain't lookin' forward to doin' my own cookin'!"

I suggested to David that he take a ton or so of salt up to

the line shack I stayed in last summer in the truck. He thought that was a good idea and added, "You can help me load it and go with me to unload it. We can take your groceries in the truck along with the pack saddles, blankets, pack bags, and whatever. We'll take it this afternoon. Then I can bring you back and I can take a load of salt up to the trap the next day. I'll take it and you can lead the horses up to your camp. I haven't moved them to their summer pasture just yet. There should be plenty of feed available up there."

"We better keep one pack saddle and a set of pack bags," I said. "I'll need something to sleep in tonight.

I kinda wished I'd have kept my mouth shut as we loaded the salt into the truck. The salt blocks only weighed fifty pounds, but the more I carried, it seemed like the heavier they got.

We finally got everything loaded. David drove to the shack and I followed in my car. We unloaded the salt and I rode back to the ranch in the truck with David.

On the way back David said, "The BLM has finally decided to build a guzzler up on the mountain. They've already started."

"What's a guzzler?" I interrupted.

"A guzzler is a big cement slab, about the size of a football field, designed to catch, trap and funnel rain water and snow into a big tank. They'll build a pipeline down to where we'll put water troughs to make it easier for the cattle to get a drink. We'll design an overflow system where, as the uppermost tank gets full, the overflow is piped down to the next tank. The whole system will consist of five water tanks scattered about four or five miles apart down the mountain. It will save a lot of water."

"Sounds like a good idea," I said. "But will it work?"

"It's worked in other states," replied David. "It ought to work here!"

"What about freezin' in the winter?" I asked.

"The pipe to each water trough will only be buried about six inches, so if it breaks in the winter, it'll be easy to spot."

"I'd put a valve every so far so the pipe can be drained in the fall an' mark it with a steel post or something. Then a feller might not have to become a plumber, lookin' for leaks an' fixin' pipe all summer."

"That's a good idea," said David. "I'll do it."

"What'll you do about keepin' trash out of the pipe?" I asked.

"They'll be a screen over the overflow pipes where they leave the trough. A feller might have to ride around and clean the leaves and debris off the screen."

"It sounds like to me that you've got this figured out pretty well," I said. "I'll be interested in checkin' it out."

"You'll see the BLM crews and some men I hired to help them as you ride out there. I go out about once a week to check their progress. They've already poured the cement and surveyed the pipeline. The men I hired are building a fence around the slab. As you ride, get acquainted with the men. There are some pretty good old boys there."

"I ain't too sociable," I said. "But I will be courteous."

The next day, I put my saddle on Bay, put a pack saddle on Stripe, haltered Blackie and Paint and set out for my camp. It was good to be back in the saddle again and in familiar country.

I made it to the line shack later in the afternoon. I unsaddled Stripe and turned the horses loose. I kept Bay saddled and after I'd put my bedroll in the cabin, rode around the horse pasture, checking fence.

There were a few places where the barbed wire sagged a little, but nothing that required immediate attention. Satisfied that the horses wouldn't get out and return to the home ranch, I rode back to the cabin, unsaddled the horse, threw him some hay and went inside to fix myself some supper.

While supper was cooking, I cleaned up the cabin. There wasn't much dust and I was surprised at that. I cleaned up the cabin enough to make it habitable for me and went out on the porch with a cup of coffee to watch the sun go down. I relaxed on the porch, contented, and forgot all about my supper and burned it.

When I smelled my supper burning, I immediately went inside and took it off the stove. I thought I could eat around the scorched part and salvage part of supper. I did some scraping and peeling, but couldn't get much. After eating what I could, I filled the pot with water, put it back on the stove, stoked up the fire and let it continue cooking. I figured I'd boil the pot clean. Trying to scrape something to eat out of the pot, I thought it might be pretty rough to try and scrub the pot clean. Still hungry, I opened a can of peaches and ate it for supper. I was full enough and the peaches helped clean the burnt taste out of my mouth.

I watched the sun go down and went to bed, my burnt meal still cooking on the stove.

The next morning I awoke to find a hole burned in the pot. I'd overcooked an empty pot! I fixed coffee and had a cup before I saddled Bay.

I gathered the horses, grained them, then caught Stripe, saddled him and turned the other horses loose.

Stripe didn't like being saddled after a long period of not being used, but I saddled him, untracked him and got on real easy. I remembered what he'd done the first time I rode him last year. I rode him around in the corral until I was fairly certain the kinks were out of him.

I rode out to see what a guzzler looked like. I saw it long before I got to it. The light-colored cement stood out in stark contrast to the gray sagebrush.

I rode up to the crew that was building fence around the cement slab. They were building a chain-link fence. The men saw me approaching and stopped working.

"You don't have to stop on my account," I said as I approached.

"It's time we took a break anyway," said one of the men. "We've been at this since before sunup."

"Chain link is pretty expensive fence to be puttin' up way out here," I said. "An' the posts bein' set in concrete will make it pretty permanent."

"It's supposed to keep all the critters out," replied the man. "I'm George Fernwood. I'm in charge of this little project."

"I'm Will. I'm ridin' for David Brown," I said. "Where's the water troughs goin' to be put?"

George pointed to the southeast. "There's a BLM crew out there surveying the pipeline and burying pipe. They'll bring up a big tank next week and hook everything up. They're only burying the pipe about six inches deep, not enough to keep it from freezing in the winter. I never could understand those government workers."

I smiled at the comment from George, but hoped the government men knew enough to put some valves in the low spots so the line could be drained before winter set in.

"I'll ride out an' see how they're comin' along," I said.

"Come by anytime," said George. "We'll be here another few days. You'll find them, they've got a couple of trucks and trailers loaded with pipe."

"I might," I said, and rode off to the southeast.

I followed the trail of the freshly buried pipe—it was easy to spot. I saw the BLM men working on the pipe. It was two-inch pipe and I figured the sections were about twenty feet long. In some spots, over rocks, the pipe wasn't buried, it was covered with other rocks. The crew was only about two miles from the cement slab when I found them.

"Howdy," I said as I rode up to them.

"Howdy back to you," replied a ranger. I recognized him as one of the BLM men that had taken the mustangs David and I had trapped the previous summer. Apparently, he recognized me.

"You riding for the Brown's again this summer?" he asked.

"Yep," I replied.

"That's good. David can always use some good help."

"What did you guys do with the mustangs we trapped last summer?" I asked.

"Some of them got adopted out, some of them went to the state prison where the prisoners halter broke and started riding them. They'll be up for adoption in another month or so. The rest went to a feedlot where they'll live out their lives, if they don't get adopted out. Have you seen any more wild horses in the area?"

"I don't know if there are any broomtails in the area. I just got up here yesterday an' haven't ridden the area," I said.

"If you trap any more, let us know. Of course you know it's against the law to run them, but trapping them is okay."

"Sure," I said. "How much pipe you got to put out an' what kind of pipe you usin'?"

"We're using plastic PVC pipe. We've got about two miles to go to get to our first trough. We don't want to start using it until the glue has dried that's holding the joints together."

"Are you puttin' in some valves so we can drain the pipe in the fall?" I asked.

"No," replied the ranger. "We've got a survey crew ahead making sure it's all downhill. It'll drain itself in the fall. A guy will just have to shut off the release valve at the guzzler tank."

"Guzzler tank?"

"Yes," said the ranger. "They'll be a big storage tank at the guzzler to collect all the water during the winter and spring. You'll just have to open the valve in the spring and the system will fill itself. It'll shut itself off after each trough gets full and open when needed. It's all gravity flow."

"It sounds like a good idea," I said. "Are you sure it will work?"

"Certainly," said the ranger. "Say, aren't you the guy that helped capture Butch Wolfe and his bunch of horse thieves?"

Reluctantly, I answered, "Yes." I didn't want the fact that I was a jailbird to get out.

"Wolfe's still in prison and facing some additional charges involving some drug smuggling," said the ranger. "Looks like he'll be there a long time. His partner from out of state was arrested earlier this spring. Some of the wild horses he had were from this area."

"That's good," I said, wanting to drop the matter.

"Are you going to testify at his trial?" asked the ranger.

"I haven't been called," I answered. "I said what I needed to say at the first trial."

"He's being tried again in conjunction with the drug smuggling. I'm surprised you haven't heard anything about it. It's big news in this part of the country."

"I haven't seen a newspaper for quite a while," I said. I was thinking I ought to send a letter to Judge McAdams telling her where I was just in case I was needed to testify. I didn't need a warrant out on me simply because nobody knew where I was.

I told the BLM man, "So long. I'll be comin' by every so often just to see how you're comin' along."

"Sure. We go to town for the weekends. I'll bring you some newspapers so you can keep track of the happenings with the horse stealers."

"Fine," I said. "What's today? Keep 'em with you. I won't be ridin' up to the trap for some time. You're camped at the trap, ain't you?"

"Today is Tuesday. The trap, is that where we met you last year?" asked the BLM man.

"Yep," I answered as I rode off.

I rode the east side of the range, checking cattle. I pushed some west. As I remembered, the west side was rougher country than the east side, but there was good feed there. The guzzler system would make it easier for the cattle to graze the west side and make good use of the feed.

I came across some of the places I'd put out salt the previous year. There wasn't any left. *I'll have to start packin' salt to-*

morrow, I thought. *That's good. Bay, Stripe, Blackie an' Spot are packin' too much weight from the lack of something to do. Soft as they are, I better take it easy on 'em.*

I rode back to the cabin and fixed myself something to eat, after feeding Stripe. I didn't sit out on the porch while I was fixing supper, last night's fiasco was still in my memory. But when supper was ready, I ate out on the porch, watching the sun go down. Supper tasted strangely like the meal I'd burned the night before, but I ate it.

The next morning I put my saddle on Bay, put pack saddles on the other three horses, loaded each one with two hundred pounds of salt and left. It would be a pretty easy day, dropping off salt at each location. I'd put out two blocks at each salt lick. That way I could keep the weight even on each horse. I didn't feel rushed to get the salt put out like I did the previous year. I knew the country pretty well.

I returned to the cabin early, turned all but one of the horses loose and relaxed the rest of the day. I wrote a letter to Judge McAdams telling her where I was and even though I was no longer on probation, I was just checking in to let her know. I'd have David mail it when he brought more supplies.

The next day I'd pack salt out to the west side, then the day after that, I'd ride fence on the west side.

Riding fence on the west side two days later, I saw a small herd of deer. I hadn't noticed many deer the year before and thought a little "red meat" might be nice for a change. However, I didn't have a gun. And the thought of being arrested by the BLM rangers for poaching a deer put that thought quickly to rest. I stopped to watch the deer run off to the timber.

I thought, *No doubt, the deer numbers would increase when the guzzler system was completed and there was more water available.*

I continued to distribute salt and fix fence the next few weeks. On some days I pushed cattle over to the west side. I did ride over to where the BLM men were assembling the guzzler pipe. The BLM ranger had a stack of newspapers like he said he'd have.

"There's some news of the Butch Wolfe developments in there," he said as he handed me the papers. "You'll have to look through all of them to find it. It's not front page news anymore."

"Thanks," I said, putting the papers in my saddlebags. "I'll look through 'em later."

We visited for a while about the progress being made on the guzzler.

"It really won't be operational until next year," said the BLM man. "We'll really need to have a good water year, a lot of snow and rain before the system will work."

"Yes," I said, smiling. "A lot of water is needed to make a water system work."

The BLM man smiled. "Yes, and that's something we don't get much of here. But we get enough to make this system work, most years."

I thanked the BLM ranger for the papers and rode off. It wouldn't be long before I'd have to move up to the trap and set up camp. I wouldn't need extra packhorses this year, David had already hauled salt to the trap. However, I didn't want to move camp too quickly. I didn't want to be camped at the trap while the BLM crew was there.

I did ride up to the guzzler one day. George Fernwood had finished putting the chain-link fence around the cement pad and he and his crew had left. There was a big galvanized tank by the guzzler and it looked like it had been hooked up. All that was needed was some water.

We did get a rainstorm, a steady, gentle rain. It rained all day. I didn't saddle up that day, I stayed in the cabin, dry, and read the newspapers that the BLM man had given me. I didn't find much about the Butch Wolfe case, although there was something about a man named Butler being arrested on drug possession and distribution charges. I didn't think much about it until I read in the last paragraph that it was suspected he was also involved with the horse stealing ring that had been arrested about a year ago. That caught my attention.

I decided I needed to amend my letter to Judge McAdams and make myself available to testify at Butler's trial if needed, even though I didn't know anything about the drugs.

A few days later David showed up with more supplies for me. As we unloaded the supplies, I told him that I might need to leave for a few days if I was called to testify at Butler's trial.

"Are you involved in drugs?" asked David, suspiciously. He'd been following the story in the paper.

"No," I answered, smiling. "But I did have something to do with capturing Butch Wolfe an' his bunch in that horse stealing ring." I didn't volunteer any more information, I didn't think David knew I was a jailbird.

"Seems like I'd heard something about that sometime ago. How were you involved?"

I thought I'd better tell David the whole story, even though it might cost me my job. So I told him how I'd hired on with Butch Wolfe as a truck driver. David smiled when I told him the part about being arrested, put on probation, and ended up caring for the horses I'd supposed to have stolen. I finished by saying, "I'm off probation an' got a clean record. The judge told me my record only showed I'd been arrested on suspicion of stealing horses and was found innocent. But I should make myself available to testify, if needed, even though I don't know Butler or anything about the drugs.

"This letter to the judge is makin' myself available if needed. I'd appreciate it if you'd mail it for me," I said, handing the letter to him. "I ain't got any change for a stamp."

"Don't worry about it," said David. "I'll mail it. You know, we lost a horse a little over a year ago, a good-looking bay horse. I thought he'd just gone off and died somewhere. Could he have been with your stolen horses?"

"That's hard to say," I replied. "There were a lot of different brands on the horses I looked after, although I did ride a good-looking, well-built bay horse while I was takin' care of the stolen horses. I don't remember any brands on him. The county took care of the branded horses and I think the brand inspector made an effort to locate the owners. Those that weren't claimed were probably sold at the auction."

"My good bay horse didn't have any brands on him," said David. "We haven't had much trouble out here."

"This horse stealing ring was supposed to have covered a lot of territory, operatin' in a few different states," I said. "It's hard to say if your horse was with 'em."

"I suppose we'll never know. Anyways, I hope he's got a good home. He was a good horse. Have you checked the guzzler to see how much water we've collected?"

"Nope," I said. "I don't think it's completed. The BLM guys didn't want to open it up until the glue holdin' the sections together has dried. I figure we got about an inch of water."

"An inch of water on that cement slab would add up to quite a sizeable amount of water. I'm curious to see how much water we collected. I think I'll go to the guzzler and check it out. Want to go?"

"Nope," I said. "I'll stay here an' fix us a noon meal."

"Oh, by the way, there's a fresh cherry pie on the front seat. Sheila made it yesterday."

"I'll be sure to get it," I said. "Seems like she sent one up last year."

"Yes, she did," said David.

Before David left, I told him, "The noon meal will be ready when you get back, although there might not be much of the pie left!"

David laughed and drove off.

I started fixing something to eat. I thought David would be gone about two hours.

David returned just as I was putting some steaks in the pan. "Dinner will be ready shortly," I said. "How do you want your steak done? Burnt? That's how I fix 'em best!"

"Medium rare," said David.

"You'll get it however it gets done!" I said.

While we were eating, I told David of my plans to move up to the trap as soon as the BLM crew left.

"I left the big tent and stove under the tarp with the salt," said David. "It's all there. You'll need to pack your groceries up horseback."

"I think I can handle it all in one trip," I said. "I'll ride over there tomorrow an' see when the BLM men are leavin'."

Disaster

When we finished eating, David made ready to leave. "I'll mail your letter first thing in the morning."

"I'd appreciate it," I said. "I'd also appreciate you not tellin' anybody I'm a jailbird."

"Why not? I think it's funny you being arrested then having to take care of the horses you were supposed to have stolen. That's hilarious!"

"It didn't seem very funny at the time," I said.

David laughed and left. I cleaned up the dishes. I saved the last piece of pie for later that night.

The next day, I saddled Blackie to ride up to the trap. He had recently been packed but when I stepped on, he started bucking. I was surprised and the horse threw me off!

I braced myself for the fall with my hands and when I hit the ground, I felt a sharp, stinging pain in my left wrist. I got up, holding my wrist. *Broken!* I thought. *That's a fine mess!* and silently cursed.

I couldn't let Blackie get away with throwing me and got back on. I couldn't use my left hand to cheek the horse or to get a hold of some mane, but managed to get on. Much to my surprise, Blackie didn't buck this time! I rode him in the corral until I was satisfied the buck was out of him. I considered going ahead to the trap, but decided my wrist needed attention.

I unsaddled the horse but kept him in the corral. I went to my car and drove to the home ranch. It took a couple of hours. When I got there, David was gone, but Sheila was there. She gave me a surprised look when I stepped on the porch.

"What are you doing here?" she asked.

"I think I broke my wrist," I said.

Sheila looked at my swollen wrist and said, "We better take you to the doctor."

"I can go. There's no need for you to leave," I said.

"No, I'll take you. I just need to leave a note for David. You go get in my car."

Her voice was very commanding and I did as she said.

On the way to town, she asked, "What happened?"

"The black horse threw me off," I said. "I tried to brace my fall."

"I never did trust that black horse!" she said.

We got to the doctor's office and after a short, but uncomfortable wait the doctor saw me. He took X-rays of my wrist and shortly came in and said, "Your wrist is not broken, just badly sprained. There's not much we can do for it until the swelling goes down. Unfortunately, sometimes a bad sprain such as this takes longer to heal than a break. About all that we can do is write out a prescription for some painkillers. You keep that wrist immobilized and it will get better. We could put it in a cast after the swelling goes down."

"I just won't use it," I said.

"You sure? If you try to use it, you could aggravate it and it will take longer to heal. You better come back when the swelling goes down and we'll cast it."

"How long before the swellin' goes down?" I asked.

"That's hard to say," said the doctor. "It might take three days or so, maybe longer."

"I can't stay in town three days," I said.

"No, you'll stay at the ranch," said Sheila.

Dejectedly, I left the doctor's office with Sheila. As we were leaving, we met David just coming into the office.

"I got your note, Sheila. How bad is it?" asked David.

"It's a bad sprain," said Sheila. "It might take some time to heal."

"Looks like you'll get a few of days off with pay, Will!"

"That don't really interest me," I said. "I need to stay busy, an' I've got to get back to the cabin. I left a horse in the corral. He'll need feedin'."

"I'll take care of that," said David. "We'd best be heading for home. Anything you need while we're in town?"

"Nope, I'm ready to go."

"We'll need to stop and get his prescription filled," said Sheila.

It was a good thing she was there, I'd already forgotten about the prescription.

We drove back to the ranch. David followed Sheila and me in the truck.

When we got to the ranch, Sheila said, "You could stay in the bunkhouse, but we've got a spare bedroom. You'll stay there. You'll get to sleep between clean sheets tonight."

"In that case, I'll need some clean clothes," I said.

"We're not going back into town for clothes shopping!" said Sheila.

"We don't have to," I said, laughing. "I've got clean clothes in the car. I'll also need a shower."

"Your room has a private bath. Will you need a towel?"

"Nope," I answered. "I've got all I need in the car."

I got a good shower that night and stayed in it probably longer than I should have, but it felt good. I even slept well in the main house, despite the sprained wrist. The painkiller prescription was working.

I woke up the next morning feeling better. The swelling in my wrist had gone down a little and I didn't feel like I needed a painkiller pill. I thought I could go back to the cabin in another day and get back to work.'

I saw David at breakfast. "I went up and turned your horse loose last night," he said.

"I appreciate that," I said. "I'll bet the horse appreciates it more!"

David laughed. "How's the wrist?" he asked.

"Better," I replied. "I can go back tomorrow. I still need to move up to the trap."

"You can't do that alone," said David. "I've been thinking. There's a high school kid that's been pestering me for a job all summer. He really wants to be a cowboy. I think I'll hire him and send him up with you to help out until your wrist gets better."

"I can handle it," I said.

"No. You'll need both hands to pack stuff and this kid is pretty stout. I'm kinda interested in getting the job done and you won't have an easy time trying to do it with one hand. I better hire this kid and make it easier on you."

"Suit yourself," I said.

The next day, the swelling in my hand had gone down considerably and a lot of the pain had left. There was still some pain when I tried to use the hand, but I could manage.

I told David and Sheila, "I don't think we'll need to cast this, I'm going up to my cabin."

"Hold on a little. I've hired that kid to help you. He should be here by noon. I thought you could take his stuff up in the car and I'd have him ride a horse and lead another up to the cabin."

"What horses you sendin' with him?"

"I'll have him ride those two I sent up as extra packhorses for you last year," replied David. "He can follow that old road to the cabin. He shouldn't get lost."

"I'll wait until he shows," I said. "Then I can get up there an' start fixin' supper. Tomorrow, I'll ride over to the trap an' see if the BLM men have left. If they have, the next day I'll move up there."

"Good," said David. "Just relax until the kid shows up."

It was difficult waiting for the youngster to arrive. When he did, he came in a car that his folks drove. He got his saddle, an old one, well used, and his bedroll from his folk's car. He also had some extra clothes in a duffle bag.

"Put your bedroll and duffle bag in Will's car," David told the youngster. "You'll ride up to the camp on one of my horses and lead another one. Oh, by the way, this is Will. He'll be your boss up in camp. Will, this is Willie Jones. He'll be your helper for the rest of the summer."

I stuck out my hand and was surprised at the grip in the young man's hand.

"How old are you, son?" I asked.

"Fourteen, sir," he replied. "I'll be fifteen in September."

"You got everythin' in the car you need?" I asked.

"Yes sir," he replied.

"Good," I said. "The sir ain't necessary. It's Will. Will an' Willie. That could become confusin' after a time. I'm goin' to head out, David. You tell young Willie here how to get to the cabin. You could ride up in the car with me Willie, but we ain't got room in the backseat for your horses!"

I got in the car and drove off, laughing at my own humorous remark.

I got to the cabin, unloaded Willie's bedroll and duffle bag and put them inside. I figured Willie would be here in about two and a half hours. We could keep his horses in overnight and use them to jingle in my saddle horses in the morning.

I didn't have anything else to do that day, so I ate the remaining piece of cherry pie that Sheila had sent up with David. It was a little old, but still good.

Shortly Willie showed up. He'd made better time than I'd figured, but his horses were covered with sweat. He came riding in with the lead rope to the horse he was leading under his saddle horses' tail. That wasn't a big thing, both horses had been packed before and were used to britchin's and the like under their tails. A feller usually only got in a jackpot when he pulled the rope hard to free it and the horse clamped his tail down. Then, it was hard to tell what would happen.

"These horses love to run," he said as he got off.

"You probably encouraged 'em," I said. I could tell he was pretty green and had a lot to learn. "Around here, we don't run the horses just for the sheer joy of runnin' 'em. We try to save their strength an' wind for when we might need it. We'll keep 'em in the corral overnight. Unsaddle your horse and turn 'em loose in the corral. Throw each one about thirty pounds of hay an' we'll see about supper. Can you cook?"

"I ain't a very good cook," said Willie.

"You might have a chance to become better up here."

I fixed up some supper and we ate. During the meal, I asked Willie to tell me something about himself. I found out that he was pretty much a city kid and had become bored in town. He loved the outdoors and wanted to spend as much time as he could outside.

"You're pretty strong," I said. "How'd you build up them muscles?"

"I work out a lot lifting weights. I haul hay for some of the farmers close to town. And I wrestle. Last year, I went to the state finals, but lost to another kid. He graduated last spring, so I figure I can take state this next year."

"Well," I said, smiling, "the only muscle you're liable to develop up here is the one you're sittin' on!"

Willie grinned. "It's all part of conditioning."

"Conditionin', huh? The horses can get in better shape, conditioned, if you will, by walkin' rather than a lot of runnin'. An' they'll get into shape faster." I was kind of upset at the way he'd brought the horses up to the cabin but had to remember that he was still just learning.

The next morning, I sent Willie out to run in the horses while I fixed breakfast. I heard the horses come into the corral before I saw them. When I looked, I noticed a saddled, riderless horse with the others. Smiling to myself, I went out and closed the gate behind the horses. I saw Willie walking toward the corral a couple of hundred yards away.

When he got there, I asked, "What happened?"

"I found the horses and they started running to the corral. My horse kicked up his hind legs and started to run after them. I fell off when he kicked up his heels."

"Are you hurt," I asked.

"Nope," replied Willie.

"We'll grain these horses, eat, and ride up to the trap."

I watched as Willie ate and wondered if there was enough food to last until David came again. We saddled horses. I had Willie ride Stripe and I rode Bay. I thought his two horses had worked hard enough yesterday.

We rode to the trap. The BLM men were just breaking their camp.

"We'll be out of here before noon," said the ranger. "I'll leave you some cement, some extra pipe and couplings that you can use to repair the pipe if it gets broke. You can cut it with a hacksaw. We reduced the size of the pipe gradually so there should be a pretty good stream coming out to the last water trough. I wouldn't start using it until next spring. That'll give the storage tank plenty of time to fill up. And the fittings should be well set by then."

"Fine," I said. "We'll be fixin' to move up here tomorrow."

"Seen any wild horses yet?"

"Nope," I replied. "I don't think they'll be any. The fence is in pretty good shape."

"Well, keep your eyes open," said the ranger. "I saw some mountain lion tracks the other day and they were fresh. You might lose a calf or two. They tend to go after the easiest prey."

"I'll keep that in mind," I said. "Maybe young Willie here would like to meet up with him. He's a wrestler!"

"I don't think so," said Willie.

We all laughed. "You call us if that mountain lion starts giving you any trouble," said the ranger. "We'd rather catch him than have him shot."

"What would you do if you caught him?" asked Willie.

"We'd probably just relocate him to another range," replied the ranger. You guys are moving your camp up here?"

"Yep," I replied

"Well, we've left you some firewood over there," said the ranger, pointing to a nice sized pile.

"We appreciate that," I said. "We'll think of you when we're burnin' it."

The ranger laughed. "You do that."

The BLM crew left and Willie and I set up the big tent and cook stove. Then we started back for the cabin. On the way, I explained what we were going to do tomorrow.

"We'll pack all the groceries and our bedrolls and bring 'em up here. That tent we just set up will be your home for the next few weeks. Then, when we've set up housekeepin' up here, we'll start our regular routine."

"You mean tent-keeping don't you?" interrupted Willie.

"I guess so. From there we'll distribute salt, fix fence, and scatter cows over the western part of the range. We'll need to be real careful packin' the horses tomorrow. It's important to get the weight on each side of the horse as even as we can. If we don't, the horses could get saddle sores."

When we got to the cabin, we unsaddled the horses, grained them, threw them some hay and went to fix our supper.

"What do you want to fix for supper?" I asked.

"I'm not much of a cook," said Willie. "How's about you fix supper and I'll clean the dishes?"

I could see that Willie was a conniver, of sorts, and I'd have to be careful that I didn't let him take advantage of me. "That sounds like a plan to me," I responded. "But the dishes had better be clean! An' that includes the pots and pans!"

The next morning Willie was still asleep when I woke up. "Willie!" I hollered. "Will! Getup!"

Willie rolled over, still half asleep. "Huh?" he asked.

"Time to get up! The day's a wastin'. You want to make breakfast or gather horses?"

"I'll gather horses," he said getting up and pulling on his pants.

"You better get started," I said. "Breakfast will be ready shortly an' we've got a lot to do today."

Willie left the cabin, pulling a coat on. The sun was already up, but it hadn't been for long.

Soon Willie returned and he was still horseback. *That's an improvement,* I thought.

He closed the gate behind the horses and came to the cabin for breakfast.

"You made it horseback this mornin'!" I said. "That's good."

"I didn't start the horses running this morning," he said.

I must have had a surprised look on my face because Willie was grinning as he said, "I was listening!"

"You might be learnin' something," I said. "We'll see how well you learn to do the breakfast dishes. I'll go down to the barn, get the pack bags an' start loadin' 'em up. When you finish the dishes, get your bedroll an' stuff ready to pack. Take everything you need, we won't be back for a couple of weeks, maybe a month or so."

I went to the barn, got the pack bags and took them to the cabin. "We'll load these pack bags pretty even," I said.

"Then take them to the barn and tie them on the horses," said Willie. He was anticipating our plan.

"I have a better idea," I said.

"What is it?"

"You'll see," I answered.

We packed all the groceries in the pack bags. When we were done, I said, "Your idea was to take these pack bags down to the barn an' load them on the horses there, right?"

"Well, yes."

152

"You can do that if you want. My idea is to go to the barn, put the pack saddles on the horses then bring the horses up here to load them. Your way or mine. You can do it any way you want. I kinda prefer to do it my way though."

"I think I like your way better. You don't mind if I do it your way, do you?"

"Certainly not," I replied. "Let's go saddle the horses."

We caught each horse and grained them. While they were eating we hobbled and saddled them. I saddled Bay with my saddle again and put a pack saddle on Stripe. I had to show Willie how to put on the hobbles and how the pack saddles went on the horses. He'd never used a britchin' before.

We got all the horses saddled then led the packhorses up to the cabin and hobbled them. We tried to get each pack bag as even in weight as we could, then put them on the pack saddles. The last things we loaded were our bedrolls.

I tied Blackie to Stripe and Spot to Blackie, using a short piece of baler twine on the end of each lead rope.

"Get on your horse," I told Willie.

Willie went to the barn and led his horse back to the cabin. He got on and I handed him the lead rope. "You can lead your other horse with your bedroll on him."

I went to the corral, got on my horse and rode him up to the cabin. I got Stripe's lead rope and started out. Willie started out alongside me.

"You just follow Spot," I said. "We don't need these horses gettin' tangled up. Stay single file."

We rode up to the trap. It was slow going, but we made it. I was glad we'd set up the tent the day before. The day was pretty well shot when we got to the trap. We unloaded the pack bags and set up housekeeping in the tent.

Willie called it "tent-keeping."

While we were eating supper, I told Willie, "Tomorrow, we'll pack salt over on the west side then the next day we'll shove some cows over there. There's a lot of good feed there that ain't bein' used."

We spent the next few days packing salt and moving cattle. Occasionally on the way back to camp, I'd drag a dead tree limb or small tree back. The first time I did it, Willie looked surprised. "What are you doing?" he asked

"We need firewood," I answered. "You can cut this to fit in the cook stove while I'm fixin' supper."

A New Menace

Our routine was pretty well set. There was riding every day, either packing salt or moving cattle. My wrist had pretty well healed and was back to normal. We continued to keep a horse in every night and turned the others out.

One morning, Willie brought the horses in and made the comment, "Something strange is going on out there. My horse was really nervous this morning and I don't know why. He acted like he was scared of something."

"Wasn't just your imagination, was it?" I asked.

"No," said Willie.

I didn't think much of Willie's comment until we rode out to move cattle that morning and came across a freshly killed deer carcass. My horse was acting a little nervous as we'd approached the carcass. Then I remembered the BLM ranger's comment about having seen some mountain lion tracks. Then I knew why Willie's horse had been nervous. He'd probably smelled the lion.

"Keep your eyes open," I told Willie. "There's a mountain lion around here somewhere."

"A mountain lion!" Willie interrupted.

"Yeah. Don't you remember the ranger told us he'd seen some tracks? I'm told they really like horsemeat. I wouldn't be surprised if we started finding some dead calves. I wish I had a rifle, if we came across him we could put a stop to his murderous ways before they got started. I'll see if David has one I can use next time I see him."

"You'd shoot him?" asked Willie.

"On sight," I answered.

Willie looked a little downhearted.

I noticed this and asked, "You're not one of them folks that believes everything has a right to life are you?"

"I ... I guess so," stammered Willie.

"Well, you can believe what you want. But look at what would happen if that lion killed one of our calves. Number one, it would deprive David of a part of his income, thereby increasing his hardship. Number two, the calf would never grow to maturity, to be slaughtered for food for how many other people? There's more hardship, for more people. Number three, it's important to remember that for every action, there's a reaction. We must always be aware that there are consequences to everything that's done, either by us or some other force."

I was surprised by my own ramblings. I really had no such idealistic ideas. My job was simply to protect the livestock entrusted to me.

I rambled on. "You really like your horses, don't you?"

"Sure," answered Willie.

"How would you feel if that lion killed one?"

"I don't guess I'd like it very much," answered Willie.

"Well, keep your eyes open. I don't want any of our cattle or horses or one of us to become prey to that lion!"

"Yes sir," said Willie, with renewed enthusiasm.

We rode on, a little more watchful of the countryside, keeping our eyes open for the lion. We didn't see him or see any more of his kills.

When David showed up a few days later with more supplies, I told him about the lion. "If I had a rifle an' see him, I could put an end to the threat right promptly," I said.

"I've got an old 30-30 at the house and some shells I could bring up next time," he said.

"I'd need a scabbard too," I said. "Of course there's no guarantee that I'd get him, but at least I'd have a chance if I saw him."

The summer wore on and we didn't see any more sign of the

lion. I didn't like carrying the rife on my saddle and after a time started leaving it in the tent when we left.

The time for school was fast approaching and Willie wasn't looking forward to it. He was becoming a pretty fair hand, paying attention to his horses and the cattle. He really liked being outdoors all the time and camping in the tent didn't seem to bother him, even as the mornings started turning a little colder. I didn't relish the coming cool fall temperatures.

One day, when David showed up, he told Willie, "Next time I come up, I need to take you back with me."

"Are you firing me?" asked Willie. "I figure I've done a pretty good job for you up here. Ask Will."

David laughed. "No, I'm not firing you. But your mother says you need to get home in time for school and buy some school clothes. School starts in another two weeks."

"Is it that close to Labor Day?" I asked.

"Yep, Will. Where have you been all summer?"

"Well, I've been right here. But I kinda lose track of what day it is. I only know that the days are gettin' a little shorter an' it's gettin' a little cooler in the mornin's. I might need to get into town an' get some new winter clothes myself."

"You can go to town anytime you want," said David. "You've been up here all summer without a day off, you deserve some time off."

"I'll probably move back to the cabin before Willie leaves. He'd be helpful breakin' camp here. We can start movin' a few cattle back to the east to make our gather easier when it comes time. There's still a lot of feed over there."

"Have you started using the guzzler yet?" asked David.

"No, we haven't had enough rain to fill the storage tank. The BLM man said we probably wouldn't get enough water to fill it until spring. We've checked it a few times this summer an' its collectin' water, but not very much."

"We need to gather a little earlier this year," said David. "I've contracted the calves and we're supposed to deliver the first of October. That means we can start gathering the first week in September."

"Can I come and help on the weekends?" asked Willie.

"Is he worth having back, Will?" David was teasing with Willie and I could see it. I thought I'd have a little fun.

"Probably," I said. "But you know he eats like a horse. If you let him come back, he probably ought to supply his own groceries! But many hands make light work!"

"You can come on the weekends," said David. "As long as you show up Friday night and be prepared to leave late Sunday night."

"I'll be here," said Willie.

"Now," said David, "when are you planning on moving back to the cabin?"

"We'll move cattle toward the east the next three days, then move back to the cabin on the fourth day," I answered.

"Then I'll be up after that, bring you more groceries and take Willie back to his ma," said David. "He should be able to start school on time."

"Will I need to ride my horses back to the home ranch?" asked Willie.

"No. Will can lead them back when he's ready. You'll ride back with me in the truck."

"I'll probably just follow you back to the ranch in my car," I said. "Then I can go to town an' get a heavier coat an' some other stuff. Besides that, my car might need a jump to get started. It ain't been run all summer."

"That's the plan then," said David. "By the way, I almost forgot, I've got a letter for you."

David went to the truck and brought a letter out and handed it to me. Reading the return address, I saw that it was from Judge McAdams. I opened it up and scanned through it. I paused and read thoroughly when I got to the part that said,

"You probably won't be needed to testify in November, but you can always stop in for a visit. You'd always be welcome."

The letter went on to tell what the weather was like and some more information. I put it in my pocket to read further when I got done with the day's work.

"Anything important?" asked David.

"No," I said. I hadn't given it any thought all summer, but was a little relieved to find out that I didn't have to go to court.

We spent the next three days moving cattle back to the east and on the fourth day we broke camp. I decided to leave the tent up, just in case we needed it in an emergency situation. We also left a sizeable amount of firewood and some canned stew and the like. The horses didn't have much to pack going back to the cabin.

We arrived at the cabin and set up housekeeping. Willie would leave tomorrow when David came up. I wouldn't have much to do, but I was sure I could do it.

I followed David back to the home ranch when he came for Willie and brought more groceries. At the ranch, Willie's folks were waiting for him.

I'd been introduced to them when they brought Willie up, but couldn't remember their names. I told Willie "so long," and shook his hand.

He said, "Thanks Will. I learned a lot from you this summer."

"Well, remember it. They'll be a written test on it next time I see you!"

Willie laughed, and I went to town. I got a motel room for the night, and bought some clean clothes, long johns for the winter, and a heavy winter coat. Later that night, I took a good long hot shower.

I got back to the ranch the next morning, dressed in some of my new clothes. When I saw David, he said, "What are you doing? You look like you're dressed to apply for a job, not ready to go back to work!"

I laughed. "I think it's good to get cleaned up every now and then. I try to do it about twice a year!"

David laughed. "You're right! You going to stay the night here?"

"I think I'll go back to the cabin," I said. "I can still ride the west side an' push cows east. That'll make our gather easier. Oh! I left the tent up at the trap. I thought it might be handy if we got caught in a snowstorm later. It would provide a little shelter in a pinch. We put a bunch of firewood and some canned goods inside."

"That's a good idea. You can go back whenever you want. We've got a few weeks until I have to deliver the calves. We can take it a little easier."

I drove back to the cabin and honked the horn as I drove into the yard. Presently the horses showed up. I grained them, kept Stripe in and turned the others loose when they finished their grain. Then I fixed my own supper.

The next few days I pushed cattle from the west side to the east side. I was done scattering salt and all the horses were getting a good rest. It was turning colder and I was beginning to get restless, ready to move on and see some new country. I would be ready to travel when we finished the fall gather.

One day, two weeks after I had gone to town, David showed up at the cabin, riding a horse and leading a packhorse with his bedroll on it. I was just saddling up when he arrived and was surprised to see him.

"What's up?" I asked. "You must have left before breakfast."

"It was still dark when I left," said David, unloading his bedroll from the packhorse. "I've decided to gather a little early. We'll keep the cattle on the hay fields and let the calves fill up a little before we ship them. It might add a little weight to them."

"They should weigh up pretty good," I said. "It's been a good summer."

"I thought we'd ride the west side thoroughly today. Then start pushing cattle toward the hay fields tomorrow. A couple of day's riding and we'll have our gather completed. Willie's supposed to show up Friday. He and Sheila will help us on Saturday. They're supposed to ride out and meet us. We should have a sizeable bunch of cows when we meet them."

"You're the boss," I said. "What's today?"

"Today's Tuesday. You really do lose track of time, don't you?"

"No need to watch a calendar up here," I said. "There's some coffee still on the stove, still hot. Want a cup before we get started?"

"Sure. I've got to put this bedroll inside anyway."

We went to the cabin and I poured David a cup of coffee. We discussed how we were going to gather cattle.

"I've been ridin' the west side pretty regular," I said. "We shouldn't find many cattle there, if we find any at all. I've been pushin' everythin' to the east. It should be a pretty easy gather, although it ain't really cold enough to make the cattle want to go home."

"We'll take them anyway. There's plenty of feed in the hay fields," said David.

David finished his coffee and we got our horses and rode to the west. We split up and made a long ride. David made the biggest circle and when we met up, sometime after noon, we hadn't gathered any cattle.

"You've done a good job clearing this west side of cattle," said David.

"I was fairly satisfied that I'd gathered all the cattle here, but it didn't hurt to make sure."

"Did you see the calf that was dead?" asked David.

"No," I said. "Where was he?"

"Way up on top," said David. "Up by the corner fence. Looked like a lion kill."

"I haven't seen any more lion signs since I came across that deer kill I told you about. I figured he'd left the country."

"They do cover a pretty big range," said David. "I'm told about two hundred and fifty square miles."

"That's probably why I haven't seen any more sign," I said.

"We'll go to the east and push everything down while we're here. Then tomorrow we'll go to the far end on the east side and push everything toward home. We'll have three days of riding, then Friday we'll start heading to the hay fields. We should meet up with Sheila and Willie about noon on Saturday."

"Sounds like a plan to me," I said.

"I wonder if that lion will follow the cattle."

"I dunno," I said. "I understand they pretty much follow the deer herds."

"I'll start packing the rifle in the truck," said David. "The deer come down in the winter. That dead calf I found, I figured he probably weighed around six hundred pounds."

We pushed cattle down the mountain. About mid-afternoon, we left the cattle and rode back to the cabin. We grained our horses and David turned his horse loose. I kept mine in so I could jingle the horses in the next morning.

"Looks like you get to fix breakfast tomorrow, while I run the horses in," I said.

"It certainly looks that way," said David. "How do you like your eggs, burnt?" he smiled as he asked the question.

"Maybe I oughta let you take my horse an' I'll cook breakfast," I said.

"I'll wait until you get back. Then you can burn your own eggs."

The next morning I ran the horses in while David cooked breakfast. After breakfast we saddled our horses and rode to the far northeastern fence. We only saw a few cows as we rode to the boundary. When we reached the boundary, we split up.

David said, "I'll pick up the cattle we passed. You take the long circle and we'll meet somewhere toward the bottom. The gates are open all the way to the highway, but the cows can't get out on the road."

We started out. The wind had picked up and the clouds forming on the other side of the West Mountains held the promise, if not the threat, of snow. It was getting colder.

I started finding a few cows and started them toward home. I wasn't finding as many as I'd hoped. It was a long ride, checking over each little rise and at the head of each draw to see if there were any cows. I'd start the cattle moving, check the surrounding area, then go back and push the cattle farther. It was tedious and time consuming, but it was part of the job.

After a few hours I saw a big cloud of dust off to the west and I figured it was David and the cattle he'd found. From the size of the dust cloud I thought he must have found a good part of the cows. The cattle I'd started had begun to mix with the herd David had found. When they were all together, we had a sizeable herd of cattle.

David rode over to me. "I missed a grand opportunity!" said David.

"How's that?"

"I saw the mountain lion, but didn't have a rifle. He was sneaking up on a little bunch of cattle that were shaded up in the aspens. He spooked when I got close and ran off. I'll start packing the rifle, even when I'm horseback from now on.

"That's strange, I haven't seen any sign of him where I was ridin'. You know," I said, "the BLM ranger said if that lion started to cause us some problems to give 'em a call. They'd come out an' trap him an' relocate him somewhere else."

"Well," said David, "there's not a phone handy out here, and it'll be a few days before I can get to one. I wish I had the rifle now!"

We pushed the cattle toward the holding pasture by the road then let them go and rode back to the cabin. It was getting progressively colder as the sun went down and I could feel it.

"I'm goin' to be wearin' that heavy coat I bought in town from now on," I said. As I said it, I felt a few raindrops on my face. "I think winter is tryin' to make an appearance. Let's move these horses out at a little faster trot so as I don't freeze to the saddle!"

"Good idea," said David.

Once we started at a trot, we made good time getting to the cabin. When we got there, we unsaddled the horses and put a nosebag of grain on them.

"If you'll pull the nosebag off my horse when he gets done eating, I'll go start supper," said David.

"Of course," I said. "If I'd have known you were goin' to cook supper, I'd have volunteered to unsaddle your horse for you! I'd do about anything to get out of doin' my own cookin'! But the havin' to eat it is the hard part!"

David was laughing as he walked to the cabin.

When I got to the cabin. David had a good fire going in the stove. The warmth felt nice.

The next day was Thursday. We'd ride the east side again today and tomorrow, then start pushing everything toward the highway, planning on meeting Sheila and Willie sometime Saturday.

When Saturday came, we started early, before the sun came up. We did find a few cows on Thursday and Friday, but not many. It had turned colder and I was glad to have my new heavy coat on. The farther we rode southeast, the more cattle we had. By the time we reached the holding pasture, we had a very sizeable herd.

As we closed the gate into the holding pasture behind the cattle, David said, "We should have met Sheila and Willie by now. I wonder where they are. I hope nothing has happened."

We pushed the cattle toward the highway. As we got closer to the road, David rode ahead to open the gate, but returned. "The gate's already open," he yelled to me. "Sheila and Willie are on the highway slowing down the traffic. Just keep pushing cattle onto the hay field."

We slowed down the herd as they went through the gate onto the highway. When the last cow had crossed the highway and entered the hay field, Sheila and Willie joined us. Willie had a new pair of chaps on.

"You and Willie were supposed to have joined us in the holding pasture. What happened?"

"The cattle had knocked the gate down and there were cows out on the highway when we got here. I thought it best to let the cows onto the hay field and stay here to slow down the traffic," said Sheila.

"That's good, but I wanted to count them onto the hay field," said David.

"You can count them into the corral," said Sheila. "At least, no one hit any of our cows!"

"Well, let's corral them now," said David. "It's only about noon, we can sort the calves off the cows. I'll count the cows into the corral."

"That's what I said," said Sheila, with a big grin on her face.

We moved the cattle to the corral and David slipped ahead to count them. When they were all in the corral and counted, David said, "We're missing about twenty head according to my count. We've made a pretty good gather. We'll sort the cows and calves today. Then tomorrow we'll sort steers and heifers. I want to select about fifty head of heifers for replacements before the buyer shows up. I've had the farm hands put out feed for the calves, we'll turn the cows out on the hay fields."

We rode back to the ranch house, turned our horses loose and called it a day.

After supper, David said, "Tomorrow we'll sort steers and heifers then select replacement heifers. I think with the guzzler operational, the range could handle another fifty head next summer. What do you think, Will?"

"It should handle that easy," I said, "maybe more."

"Then, the next day, I'll take you and your saddle back to the cabin. You can catch a horse and saddle a packhorse for your bedroll and trail the other horses home. It'll be pretty easy. Once you start the horses home, they'll pretty well come on their own. Then I'll take you back to get your car."

"We can bring my bedroll and the pack saddles back in the truck," I said. "There's no need to use a packhorse."

"You're right," said David. "I'd like to know where my mind's been lately. I guess I've been a little concerned lately—this is the first time I've consigned any calves. I hope it turns out okay."

"It'll be all right," I said. "It'll be what it's supposed to be."

"Once we get the calves loaded, your riding job will be done. But you can stay on and feed cows this winter."

"No thanks," I said. "I kinda prefer the warmer climates. I'll roll up an' move on."

"You know you've always got a job here, whenever you want," said David.

"I appreciate it," I said. "An' I'll keep it in mind."

The next few days, we worked as David had outlined. When the calves were loaded and shipped, David came to me. He had a check for the summer's wages and invited me to stay and relax for a few days before I left. He also offered me a job for the winter, again.

I declined on the offer to hang around for a few days. It was time to move on.

I didn't know where I was going, but had begun to think that working on the dude ranch in the winter, branding calves in the spring, and packing salt during the summer might not be a bad plan for the next few years. And I just have to take some time and learn how to cook!

THE END

Other Books by Stu Campbell

Horsing Around a Lot

Horsing Around the Dudes

Humor Around Horses

You Can't Be Serious!

Comedy Around the Corral

More Humor Around Horses

Muddy Waters

Comedy Around Cowboys

A Young Cowboy's Adventure Series

A Young Cowboy's Adventure

Honey

Surprise!

Intruders

Expectations

Frozen

Advice

Broken

Ginny

Wild Horses for Wild Kids

The Kids Get Horses

About the Author

Stu bases his books on his true-life experiences of ranch life and being a cowboy. He is a graduate of Utah State University with a degree in Animal Husbandry, and has also been a ski instructor, truck driver, and rancher.

About the Cover Artist

Cowboy artist, **R. Loren Schmidt**, is truly a cowboy and an artist. He illustrates from real life experiences from his lifetime of cowboying. A lifetime of dedicated art practice is evident in his expressive and accurate depictions of the contemporary cowboy experience. Loren is most inspired by his friends, horses, and the grand adventures in the backcountry of the West.